PROMISE ME A MILLION TIMES

PROMISE ME A MILLION TIMES

Keshav Aneel

Srishti
PUBLISHERS & DISTRIBUTORS

Srishti Publishers & Distributors
Registered Office: N-16, C.R. Park
New Delhi – 110 019
Corporate Office: 212A, Peacock Lane
Shahpur Jat, New Delhi – 110 049
editorial@srishtipublishers.com

First published by
Srishti Publishers & Distributors in 2016

10

Printed and bound in India

This is for you, Gagan Uncle and Aditi Di.
There hasn't been a day yet when I forgot to think of you.
I wish you both could be back!
Miss You!

A note from the author

There are no such places like Lugaar, Etiole, Bratten and Grane on earth. I have made them up because that's the thing with pure fiction – It allows you to frame things as per your taste and imagination, and relish what couldn't be or hasn't yet originally been in one place at a given period of time.

Acknowledgements

This could not have been possible without you, Merril Di. Despite the heavy workload, you on my single request, stayed awake for countless nights, going through the messy drafts of the chapters. This book, I believe, belongs to you as much as it belongs to me. And also, I can't thank you enough for the beautiful cover, designing of posters, pictures and everything that the book essentially needed.

Mom, dad…I am so indebted to you for letting me give up my job to finish this book. It was never hard to convince you to let me chase my dreams. You know your role in the making of this one. It may succeed or fail, but I will be happy, as you will be by my side like always.

I also want to show my gratitude to my teacher, Shveta ma'am. It was back in class eight, I remember, when you instilled confidence in an average doing boy with almost zero faith in self. It's because of a teacher like you that a boy who once feared sharing his opinions in a small crowd took courage to write a book.

Next, I feel immensely blessed to find some wonderful pals, who through thick and thin have always been right by my side. (So sorry for not mentioning names here. The list would have been unbelievably long, and it would be a sin to miss out even one name that has contributed to my dream coming true.)

Okay now, before I finally wrap this one up, let me reach out to my cousins. All of you have always been a massive support system and I don't really understand how to express it. I mean, being the eldest child in the family, I am supposed to be motivating and encouraging you to fight your battles, but with us, it has been the other way around. So thank you so very much for performing a role that wasn't essentially your duty at all. I love all of you. And trust me, having you all is a result of some seriously good karma.

Lastly, thank you team Srishti for this opportunity. Right from signing to editing and then to the marketing part, you have been immensely kind. It was an honour working with a house like yours.

Cheers!

Prologue

In the last twenty minutes, Edwin must have peed twenty-five times. The people sitting around noticing this, are obstreperously laughing at him. But despite his unstoppable urgency being the butt of all jokes, he is not at all embarrassed! Why? Because he has trampled like a Trojan to realize a near impossible boyhood dream. Through all those adversities that came his way, he outlasted them one by one, never giving up on his resolution. Then the hard work that he put in, and all his adherence, belief, prayers, consistency have been so commendably incredible that he has his name etched into the annals of time.

However, even after being a phoenix so difficult to become, he is quacking out of nervousness as we draw closer and closer to the results of 'The Best Actor In A Leading Role', which he, for ages, has been indescribably yearning for.

Now, after an extensive celebration of four hours, we are down to the most anticipated moment of the year. The entire movie industry and all the fans on the planet would have their attention glued to the opulent stage. The next words on the mike will echo the name of the person who will kiss the darling trophy of gold. Ed has his eyes closed. Claire has her fingers crossed. I sit behind them on one knee with my hands on their shoulders.

Every nominee has their heart pounding like never before. A beautiful lady in a sparkling gown waves and kisses the envelope from the podium that has the name in it. She is the one who is going to announce it. She is a living legend; a distinguished jury member; an all-time great.

Ed opens one eye to check the delay. He closes it back again with force. He is shivering and sweating at the same time. The lovely lady opens the envelope and smiles looking at the paper she has taken out from it. She knows the result. Yes, she does! She lifts her head up, looks at the audience, at the actors, at all the legends utterly excited. There is pin drop silence in the stadium occupied by forty thousand people.

But she just takes the other route choosing to build on the hype. She is in no mood of announcing the winner easily, and until she finally comes to doing her much-awaited part of releasing the people tightly wound on the edge of their seats, let me hold your hand and take you to the times of our beginning, or as Ed always loves to call 'those priceless times of our beginning'.

The train had paused at some station, and outside the window, it was getting hauntingly dark for an afternoon sky. Lengthy gloomy clouds were flying from west as the season awaited its first snowfall. Christmas was nearing and I, along with my best friend Edwin, was forever moving to the city of Etiole. I tried waking him up so that he could watch the flakes of snow that were beginning to drop from the everlasting roof of mother earth.

He ignored my efforts and moved towards the edge of the seat, wrapping the blanket tighter around himself and burying his face between his knees. It was not only the chill in the air but also the fatigue of travelling for the last twenty-four hours that made him so sleepy. There were dark circles under his eyes, and mine too; our faces were grubby and both of us almost looked like hippies.

An old lady with winter in her hair sat on the seat opposite to ours, and had her gaze completely fixed in a book. She, unlike me and most other travelers, was least interested in anything that was going around us. Maybe, I thought, her novel was much more interesting than the joy-triggering weather or providing her with better subjects to wonder upon than the scar on the face of the tea boy which he had been trying to cover all this time while serving the orders.

Then, as the train made a gradual movement, a young guy – definitely a little older to us – came and settled next to that old lady. He was wearing a camel coloured overcoat and underneath it was a black suit with a proper tie. His appearance was reminiscent of a quintessential guy working for the secret services department that I had painted in my mind from my favourite detective story.

He passed a warm smile as our eyes met, and asked. "So buddy, where are you heading?"

"Etiole," I replied.

"Me too," he said. "My parents sealed my fate in a bank there."

I wondered what this 'sealed my fate' was supposed to mean. "Are you like unhappy about it or something?" I finally asked.

"Well, I wanted to be a basketball player but couldn't get a scholarship."

"Bad performances on important days, I guess?"

"Not really. Well, the truth is people used their contacts and grabbed all the positions available, just as I always knew they would and expected."

"Uh! I am sorry."

My brief silence sympathized with him for a few seconds. "But hey, I think you can make a better success story this way than being a basketball player."

"Success story? And that too by working in a bank?" He smirked. "Can we please exchange our fates in that case?"

"Mine is in much worse shape than you could ever imagine."

"As in?" he asked.

"My life is like a house that has been defaced by a storms," I said.

"Can you please simplify, Mr. Shakespeare?"

"I am an orphan. And all I have is a bag of clothes and this lazy friend of mine."

"Orphan? Really? If that is the case, then I consider you supremely blessed," he retorted. "Parents are fine only to pretend to stand by you through thick and thin. And do you know why? Because it makes them eligible to fuck your ears by cursing you for the time and money they have invested in you. When in reality all that's a result of their personal insecurities and frustrations."

"Is everything you've said supposed to make me feel good or do you indeed feel that way?"

"What? About parents?" he confirmed and I nodded. "I'll prefer to have mine dead any day."

The old lady seemed to have taken offence listening to his viewpoint since she stared at this fellow as if she was going to grab him by the neck and throw him off the running train. Yet, he did not seem to be bothered and continued.

"If I decide to write my autobiography, my parents will sound worse than demons in search of human souls. It's only because of them that my basketball dreams, my venture dreams and almost every other goal that I had, were screwed. And now, it's by virtue of those retards that I will be wasting the next thirty-forty years of my life entreating people to buy some fucking mutual funds, fixed deposits and god knows what!"

I had just opened my mouth to comment when the old lady interrupted closing her book, "If a young kid like you has such thoughts, I really wonder how you'll end up."

"Like I already said, I am going to have my entire life wasted."

"And that's because of your parents, right?" The old lady's angry voice was beginning to overpower the rattling sound of the wheels.

"Of course," he said. "Had my father not settled being a janitor or studied a little more in his time or kept his god damn honesty aside, things would have been different for me."

"Sometimes we get so selfish in life, son, that we only complain about the limitations of the ones who love us. We overlook their dreams and everything they gave up for us."

"My father had no dreams, ma'am. The loser was happy being a janitor."

"In fact, he was happy loving you, you idiot. He wanted to see a moron like you grow up comfortably. And that's probably why he never mentioned his dreams to you because that's what love is. It is sacrificing without ever endorsing it. But guess what? You won't be able to understand that; love for your generation is merely a hidden propaganda, igniting from a super strong desire of getting inside the clothes of anyone you find too bang ready to be resisted."

The expression on this young guy's face clearly showed that the lady was notably right. But he didn't want to give in and humiliate himself (probably a side effect of having a massive ego).

"What about my life then?" he argued. "Should I learn to live with its ugliness? Just because this has been brought on by my father's unadvertised sufferings?"

Listening to him, the old lady stood up and took out a bottle of water out of her bag and placed it right in the middle of the seat and questioned the boy, "What do you see inside?"

"Water," he answered without thinking twice.

"Alright, what is its colour?"

"It's transparent, ma'am."

"It is, but look, this water has a certain quality. It can take on any colour you want it to take. If you want it red, you can add a red powder to it; if you want it blue, you can add a blue powder to it."

"Quite obvious," he mumbled, wondering what the lady was trying to say.

"Very similar is our life, young man. It is exactly like this water – the available colours to which, are hope and despair. If you find your life going on a flawed track, it means that you've either picked the wrong colour or added lesser quantity than required. And much more significant than this, for you to understand is, that there is a vast difference between hoping to succeed and almost hoping to succeed. When we expect to fulfill our goals, it requires sheer absence of doubt, bringing an audacious shot without brooding over the probability of failure. However, when the element of dubiety crawls in, like in your case when you said you knew people were going to employ approach, your devotion must have lacked there, and that stopped you from pushing your limits. And addressing your disappointment, it isn't the side-effect of failing, because failures disappoint nobody. Wasting opportunities, finding poor excuses and blaming your loved ones does that."

"It is very easy to rip apart someone's life. Form an impression about anybody you meet and tell them how it could have been," the young fellow growled looking at me.

"My point, my dear son is: the way you crib won't magnify the sympathy you get, but will only assist others in classifying your character. Look, everybody in this world is going to have their own share of problems, and this is perhaps how life works – losing your compulsory battles, the people you love...or maybe each and every single thing you have. But despite all the adversity you go through, happiness requires no materialistic set-ups; it only demands not being blinded by your limited perception of the world, that's it."

I don't really know whether the guy was pissed off hearing the same thing over and over again, or finding it hard to acknowledge the truth, but whatever it was, he immediately got up and moved to another seat. The old lady shook her head, agonized or whatever, and without wasting any more time and energy, she went back to reading the book.

The train then entered a lengthy tunnel, and when it came out, the sight outside the window had switched from vast fields and dark walls to wide roads that were flooded with a caravan of monstrous trucks.

Finally after twenty-five hours of leaving everything back in Lugaar, we were about to reach Etiole. Almost all of our childhood had been lost in the hidden darkness of an orphanage, but this one dream of my friend – of being on that thirty-five mm screen – could indeed shape our destiny. I was confident that my friend's dedication would stand amongst those stories that would become a shining example of how a common fate transformed into a remarkable lifetime.

Edwin got up yawning heavily, feeling the downturn in the train's velocity. I lifted the window cover again to notice the swirling rays of the sun fighting their way through the moving clouds.

"How strange nature is," the old lady stated. "A few miles back it was snowing, and here, there isn't even a faint trace of it."

I couldn't have agreed more.

Then, as the train came to a complete stop, we stepped off, feeling exceedingly welcomed in the most aesthetic land we had ever seen. Our eyeballs froze at the astonishing lattice work and the giant glass roof spread generously around everywhere. There was a bronze statue of Christ right in front of the escalators that took us to a bridge, and on the opposite side, there was a tiny botanical garden in front of the other escalators, bringing passengers down to the principal platform. Surprisingly, there were no hawkers and vendors to be seen. Instead, there were proper outlets for everything. We were amazed to see, how despite of long queues, people stood so patiently at the booking counter. A colossal hour glass in the middle of reservations and enquiry section formed the major point of attraction. To avoid any human touch, steel poles with chains running through them stood as guards in the shape of a pentagon.

It was getting dark outside, and it definitely wasn't an appropriate hour to go and hunt for a room. We therefore tried looking for a temporary place to settle down inside the station itself. While fishing for it, we saw a number of men and women who were busy taking care of the cleanliness. Many of them looked old and fragile to be bearing such heavy tasks on their shoulders.

A mirrored pillar had a name in capital golden letters of the person who had inaugurated the station three decades ago. It made no sense to me. Rather, it disgusted me. I failed to understand why I was effortlessly able to explore the name of someone who merely inaugurated a significant public spot, but nowhere could I locate a mere token of respect for those, who gave their entire life preserving the pulchritude of the place by keeping it clean and unblemished.

We searched for some sort of a place to rest our heads, but unable to find one, I asked a passer-by if he could suggest me a concourse to sleep. He sniggered at me saying, "Go to the waiting room, strange fellow."

This wasn't what we had expected. I mean, there was this big open space inside the railway station of our village where anyone could sleep or stay as long as they wanted. But here, things were too different.

Unable to think of any other option, we took route to the waiting room. Seeing the cop only allowing the passengers with tickets for the trains yet to come, we took our steps back. We wanted a shelter for ourselves but the question now was where do we find one? Hotel? No, it would be way too pricey. May be a bus stop? Oh, yeah! We could certainly crash in a bus, one that was vacant and not starting its journey until the next morning. I asked Ed if we should catch a cab to reach the nearest bus terminal, but he wanted to walk as his legs were stiff from sitting the whole day inside the train. We checked the city map to locate the nearest bus terminal, but it was a little faded thereby making it difficult to understand the directions. One of the security personnel standing outside an ATM nearby came to our rescue, explaining the way through the alien streets of Etiole.

As we made an exit and began strolling through the wide pathways, our heads rolled back, noticing the neo-classical design at the entrance of the station. The façade was decorated by statues of unforgiving warriors, followed by the multiplying wonderment of the monolithic skyscrapers which were built incorporating different cultural and historical patterns. There surely must have been thousands of windows, for each building shimmered like exquisite mirrors. I wondered who had braved those heights every day to keep those windows so clean. The giant light poles on roads throwing golden light on them stood like guardians of the universe with arms fully stretched and a fireball in each hand to show the way to their army. On every turnaround there were fountains, enchantingly jetting water into the air. The tiny droplets would fly and fall on passersby, making everything feel all the more adorable and cute.

We had covered a handsome distance and weren't even bothered about the course we were taking. There was music in the streets, culture in air and a ravishing glamour in the attire of people. Art galleries, grand cathedrals, museums and the innumerable prolific eccentricities like clock sculptures, high end shopping arcades and traditional chariots compounded the magnetism of the place. The city was dominatingly adorned by an exceptional sense of creative achievement. To add more to its obsession, there were innumerable buskers amusing the encircling crowds with incredible skills like sword swallowing, contortions, circus acts, and more. The one that tempted me the most was a long-faced man playing four instruments all at same time with unbelievable adroitness.

We were also spellbound by opulent cars and bikes – a sight that was never available back in our village. It was an experience in itself to hear the roaring sounds of their smooth engines.

"Someday, we too are going to own that, Charlie," Edwin said, watching an M6 Gran Coupe passing us by. Our eyes never left it as it glided like a wonder on the road.

"This stuff should motivate us, Charlie. This is what we have come here to earn."

"I believe in you, brother," I uttered with aplomb, my eyes still frozen to that black sweetheart.

"Either own it to make green with envy those who have all luxuries in life, or earmark these ritzy products as inspiration to conquer your ambitions. It's in our hands, isn't it?" Ed said as we began to walk again.

"With no one to support you in the fierce competition of the film world, conquering would not only bring these babies, it would carry immortality along too."

"And may I ask what makes you say so?"

"I believe there are two things about success: the one achieved with help is appreciated, but the one achieved without it is worshipped."

"You mean, I'll be a God one day?"

"You will always be my bitch, you foul dork," I said kicking his butt and then putting my arm around his shoulder.

After walking a few more absorbed steps in overwhelming wonderment of the place, we paused before a restaurant that gave away a Victorian-esque kind of charm. It was packed with people and we had to wait for about twenty minutes before latching on to freed chairs and forthrightly requesting for the menu. After taking a brief look at it, I turned the menu towards Ed, drawing his attention towards the price column. The cheapest food at the restaurant was almost equal to the price of five to six dinners we could have afforded back in our village. After a long debate over the feasibility of dining at such an expensive restaurant, we eventually decided to go for it, partly because both of us were terribly hungry and partly because it was a moment to celebrate our friendship.

Reaching the conclusion of a fried fish being the most suited to a Lug's (person of Lugaar) taste buds, we waited for our order staring at the beautiful young ladies in the place. A boy holding his pants in his hands and a girl with her head down, trying to control her smile were being escorted out by a couple of bouncers. A guy seated next to our table seeing this commented, "What a slut to ride!"

Edwin immediately snapped, "Would you say the same for your sister?"

The guy jumped out of his seat aiming to take the exchange of words to another level, but soon settled down as people around us started to intervene and tried to calm things down, asking us to focus on our food.

After having a meal whose quantity was more or less like a sensible report on a bad news channel, we moved out with our guts still rumbling in hunger. We then hailed a taxi that had just stopped on the other side of the road. Crossing quickly, we reached the taxi and tapped the window and asked the cabbie to take us to the nearest bus station as we were too tired to walk anymore.

After ten minutes of riding in the taxi, we stopped outside an ultra-modern steel structure, designed mainly as overlapping bars. Quite apparently, this was going to be another mould-breaking piece of phenomenal architecture, comprehensively able to distinguish itself from all the insipid concrete sheds, better avoided for the stink of the public toilets.

Stepping inside, we were astonished by the transparent wing-shaped roofs of all the terminals and all the blue double-decker buses looking new and freshly painted. Even more surprising was a considerable rush of people even at this odd hour of the night. There must have been about seventy to eighty people still out in such freezing weather.

I looked at the clock and it was almost past midnight. Noticing the foil-coloured slung benches, adjacent to every bus-bay, I suggested they wouldn't be a bad option to sleep on. We threw our bags on those seats followed by our fatigued bodies, only to hear a sharp sound of whistle getting louder and louder. We looked around to check and saw a cop running towards us, gesturing us to get up.

"Out of this place!" he screamed at us.

We thought of calmly explaining our situation or bribing him, in case it got worse. However, as he came close to us, he aggressively swung his thick stick and before the wood could redden our flesh and crack our bones, we instantly dashed from the scene.

"Where do we sleep, Charlie?" Ed asked, tired and sleepy. "Should we go to a hotel?"

"Probably. We have no other option now."

We kept navigating through the city in search of a decent hotel. But sadly, neither did we come across any hotel that suited our budget or accommodate us this late in the night, nor was there a single human being around to help out with an address around the city. The speed of our marching footsteps declined continuously; we were on the verge of collapsing within a few seconds. The fluttering street lamps, the sound of planes, the heavenly rustle and stillness of all the day dominating pother offered but no consolation. Finally, a smile appeared on our faces seeing a few people sleeping under a segmental bridge that was a few steps ahead of us.

"I guess these people won't mind if we join them. What do you reckon, mate?" I asked Edwin who by this time looked completely out of energy.

"It's not a candle light dinner, buddy; it's a street light slumber fest. Why would they mind?" He said, marching towards the bridge, not waiting for me to make a move.

Without caring about the muddy ground and the thickening layer of fog, we sipped in some alcohol to keep our bodies warm, then layered ourselves with as many clothes as we could, made pillows out of our bags and lay in the hope of being able to catch some sleep.

"Good night, Charlie."

"What is so good about this night?"

'Our togetherness, buddy."

"Oh! Yeah," I softly said, drowning in sleep.

"Charlie, do you see that beautiful building with the board 'Eden Apartments'"?

"Yeah, is it calling you to come?" I asked, unwilling to take the pain to look at it through the slowly thickening fog.

"One day we will have a room in that edifice. Every evening, we will look towards this place through its window and celebrate how we stood by each other during bad times."

"And slept too, buddy. Don't forget that," I said, planting a soft kiss on his cheeks.

"Etiole seems to have improved your sense of humor," he said, wiping the moisture.

"I hope it enriches our bank account too."

"Bank account? Well said, mate." His voice suggested he was close to sleep.

Our first night in the city was not unlike what I had expected it to be. Yes, I knew that we were going to struggle for food and shelter on reaching, but experiencing it was different than all the images that I had woven in my mind. Ed's snoring began, and it did not let me close my eyes for even a moment. I thought of executing my home made remedy of twisting his nose sharply, but thought against it as I knew he was worn out. Instead, I got up and lay against a round cement pillar. The ground there was like a forty-five degree slope, robbed of its share of mud. I shifted left and right and tried hard to sleep but failed each time. My body had gone stiff like a dark board, and I was finding it extremely difficult to make the slightest of movements.

I must have somehow fallen asleep at some point as the sky, I found on waking up, was not black anymore. The sounds of horns and engines had begun to fill the air, and everyone sleeping around us the previous night was already gone.

I got up, woke Ed, and together we decided to find a place to eat and prepare ourselves for the day. We discovered a decent food court, but first rushed to its washroom to have mercy on ourselves. The tap seemed like a treasure trove, and the water gave us freshness like never before. We then took the vacant chairs by the corner and ordered ourselves breakfast. The place had only few a people seated, and those I could figure, were probably tourists.

I glanced over and over again at a mother seated next to us, lovingly making her little daughter eat. The girl would take one bite of the food and go round and round the table singing and dancing, and as soon as she gulped the bite, her mother would stop her to give her another. Not only was the girl gleefully having it, but the contentment the mother received after making her child eat was evident and shining on her face. How complete their world seemed to be! A moment of safety in my mother's arms was a wish that was never going to get fulfilled. When I was of that girl's age, I had no one in my life for whom my smile could have meant something. No one chased me around to ensure that I didn't remain hungry. No one ever watched my innocent games and took me in their arms to make me feel safe.

Lucky are the people who have families, and it's so nice to value them and to be valued back. Yet, much of the world doesn't realize this until they lose them or it's too late.

I had tears welling up in my eyes. I was missing my mother about whom I knew nothing. Edwin was sharp to realize the emotions I was going through. Therefore, he quickly diverted my attention by dragging me along with him to enquire about the areas where we could find a room.

Our first day in Etiole was proving as disappointing as the previous night. The first few rooms we saw were good, but the rent proved to be a major obstacle. Moreover the areas that we ended up in our search for affordable shelter never looked to be in synchronization with the city that had mesmerized us the previous night. These areas in contrast had congested streets and small unpainted buildings set next to each other and built much tastelessly. Cracks were wide and visible, clothes were hanging in balconies and plants were bending out of their pots, completely uncared for.

Five hours had passed in a similar fashion – going in and out of houses watching the same structures and bland walls over and over again. We were leaving the seventh house for the day, disappointed and taking course towards the next one when we heard someone calling us from behind. We turned to see a red-haired fellow with frog-like eyes rushing towards us in long strides.

"Hey, my name is Max," he said, extending his hand.

"I am Charlie," I said, taking his extended hand in response.

"If I am not wrong, you are looking for a room, right?"

"Yeah. Can you help us?" Ed asked.

"I live in a rented flat. Currently four guys are occupying it and we got place for two more. The total rent is pretty high, but the more the people, less each one's share. So, if you guys don't mind, you can join us."

"That would be awesome," I said.

Edwin though agreed with me to check out the room, his disappointment was clear and I could see that he was too tired to have a look at another house and come back empty handed. I couldn't blame him, but the red-haired guy was the last option for the day as we both were not sure about finding another roadside space to spend the night.

The red-haired guy took us to a housing complex that seemed to be squeezed between two giant buildings. The room he mentioned was on the topmost floor. The stairs were abnormally small in width, requiring us to take each step carefully, and the corridor was so dark and quiet that for a moment we felt like we had been conned into a cave. As Max unlocked the door and pushed it open, the level of cleanliness left us shocked. Plastic bags, bottles, leftovers, packets, used napkins, wet shoes and dirty socks were lying all over the floor. There was no bed, but two mattresses that stood against the wall and four white plastic chairs tossed around, adding to the overall chaos. It seemed as though the flat was inhabited by some dangerous wild animals.

It was a complete role reversal as Edwin who half-heartedly had come was now running on his own around the place, checking everything from top to bottom as if he had suddenly discovered the lost Atlantis. While I stood still, wondering if we should take up the offer.

Max then gladly described the other inhabitants and the sleeping arrangements that they followed. The whole place was just an extended matchbox with one giant room that coupled as the bedroom and living room. There were two other rooms which were so tiny that stretching your hand would mean hitting the wall. But thankfully, there were two beds and a wooden cupboard in each one of them.

Ed seemed to have already made up his mind on moving into the place so when Max asked whether we were interested, I had to reluctantly nod yes. Since we both had barely any luggage with us, there was no moving in ceremony that was required. As soon as we had dumped our luggage in the corner, we had officially made ourselves the new tenants in the place.

Max left for his office shortly and we carried on with unpacking whatever meager belongings we had with us and settling ourselves in the new house. Time flew quickly as the charm of another cloudy day made way for a peaceful evening, soothing us to a beautiful sleep. But before I could completely fall into a deep slumber, I heard the doorbell ringing so persistently that for a moment it felt like it was knocking against my head.

I dragged myself out of bed and opened the door. There stood a dark guy, looking confused upon seeing me. He moved a few steps back to check the flat number, made sure it was the right one and then scanned me from top to bottom while I stood there watching him in amusement.

"Who are you?" he asked while cautiously entering the flat.

"I am Charlie, new tenant. Max, the red-haired guy brought us here."

"Oh!" His suspicion melted into a greeting. "It's always great to come across a new mate," he continued, shaking hands with me. "I am Johnny by the way. Jonathan Samuels."

"My name is Charlie."

"Great," he said, dropping his bag against the wall. "So where are you from? Etiole itself?"

"No. No. I am from Lugaar."

"Lugaar?"

"It's a small village on the border."

"So you came here in search of a better life like the rest of them?"

"Yeah, you can say that."

Something about what I said had tickled his funny bone because he gave a very hearty laugh.

"I work as a salesman in a publishing company; if I can be of any help, I'll be glad to," he offered.

"I am really glad to meet you," I acknowledged. Before he could throw another question at me, I told him that there was another guy with me who'd be sharing the flat, thus excusing myself for a moment and hurrying inside to wake Ed up.

He, however, was too lazy to bother.

"Come out man, there is a guy waiting outside for you," I said, irritated as he ignored all my attempts.

"Who?" he probed, half awake, "Who is waiting for me?"

"The other bloke who stays here, you jerk," I almost shouted

He apathetically got up, scratching his head and following me outside. As Jonathan saw Ed coming, he had a wide welcoming smile on his face and stood up from the mattress to greet him. Both of them introduced themselves only to be interrupted by the door-bell ringing once again.

"I will get that," Jonathan said, walking to open the door.

A guy rushed in and made a run for the bathroom without even noticing us while another guy followed him, laughing and yelling at him, "That's why I keep telling you to control your eating, bitch."

Before he could be surprised by our presence, Jonathan informed him that we were the new tenants and would be sharing the flat with them.

"Perfect," he said as he came towards us to shake our hands.

"My name is Benoit Right and the guy who just rushed to the bathroom is Eugene Left. We are twins, known as left-right," he said.

It was awkward yet hilarious, but even more hilarious was the logic behind the name. Benoit explained how the twins decided that one would comb his hair from the right side and other from the left to avoid any confusion since both of them were absolutely identical.

"So, I guess you all have met each other?"

We turned to see Max walking through the door which was still left open. The joy on his face reflected the impeccable day he had had at work.

"How's work going on, brother?" Jonathan asked

"It's quite palpable from his face. You needn't ask him, Johnny," Benoit said.

"He is hardly joyous due to a favorable day at work, buddy. I guess he must have met Laura today," Jonathan commented.

"It was a demanding day at work," Max clarified, jogging to the fridge to pick an apple. "I am fucking far from my targets, and yes you are right Johnny, I was insanely off until I met Laura."

"I am craving for wine, pig heads. How about a little party?" Eugene shouted as he came out dancing from the washroom. I was dazed to see how similar he and Benoit looked. There was not even a tiny disparity in the facial features. Both of them were carbon copies of each other.

"We have no reason not to party guys. So, shall we?" Jonathan said, addressing no one in particular.

"But where the hell do we go?" Max asked

"Chaste City. The place will be raining with hot girls," Eugene said, rubbing his hands in excitement.

"Chaste City? How far is it from Etiole?" I asked, unwilling to travel.

Everybody in the room chuckled while Ed and I looked at each other in bewilderment.

"It's just named 'city' but is not an actual city," Max said looking at our confused faces. "Don't worry you will know more when we reach there. So we better head out before the place gets packed for the night."

Since Edwin and I were the first ones to get ready, we waited in the hall for everyone else to come out. We were in sober clothès while all of them were immaculately dressed in blazers and tapered jeans. My perception of being in the same financial league with all of them fell like a house of cards.

"We cannot leave like this," Johnny mumbled, shooting a look at our clothes.

"Any...anything...wr...wrong?' Edwin asked, stammering in embarrassment.

"You guys must dress up neatly. We are going to an exclusive place," Eugene advised.

I apologized admitting that most of our clothes were of the same kind – old and faded. Their slightly open mouths were enough to convey that they were feeling awkward or ashamed to take us along. So we requested them to go ahead while we would stay back and would accompany them some other day. The guys, however, didn't listen to us.

"My size should fit both of you. Come with me," Max said, making us follow him.

He took out all his blazers, offering us to choose from them. It was the first time that I was wearing such a light weight jacket. I took a look at myself in the mirror, and God! I was looking better than ever before.

The guys were smoking cigarettes in the hall when we came out. A loud roar of appreciation rose seeing us in our new attire. They made us feel comfortable about ourselves and the feeling that we definitely belonged to their group.

I stood curiously, staring at the huge rectangular glass windows of the metro train that we had boarded. Most of the platforms that the train stopped at were so intimidatingly occupied that I unconsciously gripped the pole to prevent being pushed by all the people entering and exiting. The crowds seemed to be swatting me away from their path as if I was some kind of an unwanted fly. After having passed through some incredibly long tunnels and several metro stations, we arrived at our final destination.

Max was right that the place wasn't a different city, but nothing about Chaste City was less in grandeur that an elaborate city stretch would have. It was basically a mini city with various malls and eating joints, all vying for attention. In the center of it was a silver coloured building that was lit up like a birthday cake .The place screamed elegance and serious money.

I noticed a long line of people who were dressed to the nines and waiting to be let inside. It was the presence of young blood – the way they carried themselves, their neat hair styles, the shine on their faces, the unmatchable energy in their body language – that made me so strongly crave to have my destiny shaped like one of them. They were classy, looked rich – in fact, very rich – and seemed to be enjoying themselves to the core. I felt as if that was what you would call life, and certainly not the one that I had experienced through the years.

Thinking about all this stuff and looking around in envy and desire, I silently followed the gang into a silvery lift that took us to the top floor of a building. According to Max, it housed one of the finest bars in our country.

The emphatic sounds of hands and feet of people dancing on the floor created a pandemonium. Laser beams drew quickly changing patterns, complementing the beats of music. Our IDs were checked and we made our way rubbing and pressing through many sweaty bodies that were swaying to the music. The holistically designed metal seats and rectangular tables added a touch of stimulating beauty to the place. Our orders began to speed up as Right-Left announced that they would be paying on behalf of each one of us. The combination of wine and professional exasperations (as termed by Max) made people dance without caring much about what the world conceived of their performances.

I was closely observing that the sparkle and verve every person dispensed was increasing as the night grew older. While others were spinning to the tunes of loud music and enjoying the sumptuous eatables in between, I was longing for peace. Why? Maybe because I was designed to be a loner, or maybe because the habit that had been inculcated from my helplessness of being alone was taking over me. Finally, when I couldn't bear the deafening sound, I excused myself from the group and got up to find some place to be alone.

Minding my way, I noticed a girl sitting on a long chair wearing a moonlight coloured dress. I could only see her from one side so I tried switching my position to a better angle. Her beautiful hazel eyes were like an ocean at peace. Someone placed a party hat on her head and she looked even prettier. The expressions she had on her face were like awe-inspiring tricks of a conjurer, making smiles drizzle all over the world. As she blew the candles on a cake, I began to clap and sing along with all her friends. I hadn't realized that I was standing right in middle of the place until everybody around me started bursting into laughter. But I did not care, and I was not embarrassed. She was that beautiful. She was that pure!

"Where were you?" I ignored the familiar voice.

"Where were you?" The same voice repeated.

"Where were you lost, you idiot?" I felt a strong hand on my shoulder, and immediately turned to see Edwin standing bewildered.

"I was going to the restroom, I told you guys," I said.

"Then why are you standing here in the middle of the bar and clapping?"

I looked here and there in confusion, searching for words. But in the end, rushed back to my table for I did not know what to say. There was no one sitting there, but as soon as I took a seat, Edwin joined me and stared at me without blinking. I smiled and took my eyes off him, grabbing my drink and thinking about the girl in my mind.

Meanwhile, the people around continued to go bonkers. Nobody cared how comical they appeared. They weren't here to be judged. They were here to shake the ghosts out of their mortal bodies. Benoit came and insisted that I join them all on the dance floor. I refused saying that I had a terrible pain in my legs, which was honestly a big lie as my interest in dancing was blown apart by that attractive girl celebrating her birthday.

I wanted to see her again, or may be talk to her, but lacked the courage to do it.

I kept making brisk movements on my chair to catch a glimpse of her, but the crowd, time and again, kept interrupting my view. And when they finally cleared the spot, she had gone. I kind of felt bad about not being able to catch another glimpse of that girl, but then it was time for us to leave too.

"Let's have a cup of tea," Eugene proposed, leading us into a famous oolong tea shop right next to the exit door on the ground floor of the mall.

"None for me," Benoit said as we all sat down.

"Why? Don't you like tea?" Edwin asked.

"I do, but I don't drink tea anymore."

"Why?" Edwin was surprised.

Benoit's only answer was a shrug so I pushed him to answer in words; his gesture gave a clear indication of some story being behind him quitting tea.

"Come on, we have met two new wonderful friends, so let this be the day you finally come out with the story," Max said.

"Story, is it?" I whispered.

"Guys, I don't like to talk about it."

"I am sorry, Benoit. I won't push you. But in case you share it, none of us would make fun of you," I promised.

"It's not a funny incident," he said.

"Then you must not hold it back anymore," Max insisted.

Pondering over it for a moment, he finally agreed.

"Well, till three years back, I used to drink a lot of tea. On an average I used to have ten to twelve cups every day. It was the evening of the 31st of December 1998 when I was sitting in this very place with my girlfriend Jessica, having tea with her and pressing mind over what my New Year resolution should be. I said to her I would never have tea again. She laughed at this, vouching that my resolution was soon going to fall apart as I was a huge tea addict and asked me to commit that whenever I would break it, the first cup of tea I would have would be made by her. I promised and assured her to be ready with a nice cup within a week. Two days later, Jessica died in an accident, and I never had the heart to break my promise to her or to touch another cup of tea ever. I guess…I guess she must be waiting for me in the heavens to make me that first cup."

He had big tears in his eyes that slipped treacherously onto his cheeks and lightened the agony he was hiding in his heart.

"We all shall have it only when Jessica makes one for each of us," Ed declared and got up straight away.

A similar gesture from everyone – a profound agreement to what Edwin said revealed how much they loved him. Benoit pleaded us to not pledge anything, but none of us listened to him. And why would we? Because after all, this is what friendship is truly about. When we aren't capable enough to defeat the afflictions of our friends, we must at least choose to not let them stand alone in its face. Okay, maybe it won't lessen their pain, but it surely gives them that much needed help to survive. And that's what the most important thing really is. That's what life really is.

We reached our rooms and crashed almost instantly. It was, by all means, a very extensive night for me. I had gone to a place that was truly magnificent, had the finest beer, listened to the pain of a friend that he had never shared before, made a promise that I meant to keep whole-heartedly and somewhere in between, glimpses of the girl kept popping before my eyes.

The next morning, we all got up a little late. It was perhaps another cold day and I strongly wished to stay inside the blanket but we had plans that had to be taken care of to start our journey in Etiole. As soon as we got out of our beds, Ed and I noticed something hilarious happening. Eugene's stomach had decided to misbehave all of a sudden, and he ran around howling like a wounded puppy with deadly farts drilling through our nostrils and contaminating our divine lungs.

On the other hand, Jonathan had silently taken off with Max's clothes that he had so passionately ironed and had looked forward to wear that day. Meanwhile, Benoit came out of the washroom covered in soap, wrapped in a mere towel to cover his modesty, complaining that the water supply had stopped. He ran all over the place in his towel and soap dripping, leaving the floor greasy. And Max, who had just worn another pair of ironed clothes, slipped on the floor, clonking his hips like barn door on a twister.

I said to Ed, laughing, "In case I manage to find a job, I better be up before all of them."

"But," he replied, "First go find one."

It was the previous night that Johnny had suggested a job in sales would be apt for me as it could bring huge incentives besides the regular income. Therefore, he gave me the address of a pharmacy company to check for a suitable vacancy. I decided to listen to his suggestion and check out the company. In spite of saying no, Edwin accompanied me to the office, which was a relief; having him with me, it was much easier to find out the directions and to block out all the nervousness that accompanied my first job hunting quest in the city

It had begun to snow outside, and everything on the roads of Etiole had slowed down – the trucks, the cars, the metro and life itself. The address that Johnny had given was located in an edifice of a hundred other offices. It was funny how walking through the doors of the office had suddenly brought back the memories of the girl from last night and I couldn't stop thinking how magical it would be to find that girl over here, in this very office we had just entered.

At the reception, we met a middle-aged person who requested us to wait for some time while he was busy playing with the keys of his computer. We sat on a giant black couch that was placed opposite the reception desk. We had been waiting for quite a while and out of boredom, I picked several newspapers that lay in front of us, and began flipping through them. I stumbled upon the pictures of regular protestants up to something new, a hot president of some international agency, the fanatic Prime Minister of our neighboring country, an actress who had recently had a plastic surgery and some big names from a soccer team who had threatened to boycott the coming international championships. With no interest in reading any news pertaining to any of them, I kept the papers back in their place. We then spent the next hour looking at the imposing aquarium of water-dwelling plants and guppies, placed exactly to the left of our sitting place.

My mind started revolving around those tiny creatures whose world was confined to that glass box. Wasn't it a jail for them? I wondered. Did those creatures ever have the opportunity to live in the natural world, and if that was so, how miserable would they be feeling inside the tank? Perhaps in their own pretty language they must be supplicating everyone they saw to release them.

"Excuse me."

A fromally dressed, abnormally tall lady broke the chain of thoughts running in my head, asking me to join her in the meeting room.

I marched behind her, crossing many working in their respective cabins, and feeling as if they were machines and not human beings. They all looked so dull, so depressing – programmed to work in an instructed way, in a particular manner only, and not break that fold.

I followed the lady to a cabin in the corner of the office space while Ed waited for me at the reception. It was clearly positioned in a way that the person sitting inside the cabin could see every corner and person in the office. The place was filled with graphs, motivational wallpapers and achievements framed in golden frames and placed in such a way that they were the first things that one would notice while entering the cabin.

"I see no reason choosing you for this job. However, since the festival season is coming up and many of our employees have already given their leave applications, we are in urgent need of a salesman. So I'll keep you with us for a month. If you perform well, you stay on, or else you will be asked to leave."

I was amazed at how straightforward the lady was. I had barely taken the seat when she had already taken a glance at my resume and decided to offer me the job, at the same time making sure that she was doing me a huge favor.

"Be at the office tomorrow by nine. Your team leader will be there to guide you."

While she kept telling me more about the rules and regulations, I had completely zoned out. I wondered whether it was pure luck or was it that easy to land a job. The lady was on a spree talking about what I should do and shouldn't and after what I felt was an hour of rules and regulations being hammered into my brain, I walked out of the cabin to an eagerly waiting Ed.

Ed jumped in joy as soon as he heard about what had happened. But I, I was apprehensive about being able to keep the job for long as I was a school dropout. Also, I wasn't sure of being able to survive in a world that valued the list of successful business deals one cracks rather than how the person cracks them. I had grown up working in Ben's Bakery where we mingled and dealt with our customers as friends, sharing their joy and sorrows whenever they dropped in. Coming from such a place, I was not sure of surviving in one where there were only potential clients and nothing else.

Ed, on the other hand, was getting prepared to chase his dreams as the following day he decided to go and get his portfolio made for movie and serial auditions.

A real formidable time lay ahead of us, and the future, well who knew what was going to happen!

Ever since I joined my new office, Salud Pharmaceuticals, there was one thing that was repeated to me over and over again: the company had built its reputation over a series of decades and as an employee, it was my responsibility to maintain it while dealing with customers. We had to be at our best-dressed to the nines, clean shaven, in formal clothes, and supremely neat.

My role was to visit all pharmacy stores inside various hospitals of the city and persuade them to buy our company's medicines. I was to make sure that I maintained a certain amount of sales every month, above which incentives were assured. But at the same time, if there was anything lower than the intended figure, I was going to be fired. I also happened to find out that I was doing an illegal job when I was given strict instructions that in case anyone asked me about my qualifications, I must say that I had done studies in pharmacy or else I could end up in jail.

The anxiety about getting caught was hovering in my mind when I entered the first hospital as a new sales coordinator. I stood there in the parking lot of the hospital, contemplating questions like: what if I am asked questions about my pharmacy credentials? What if I sold a wrong drug and the same was consumed by a patient? Even worse, what if the patient died because of it? For a minute, I had almost decided to run away, but somehow in the end, a divine intervention put me on the track to start off with my work.

An unusual rotten stench left me stifled on entering the hospital building. I turned around hearing an ambulance hooter creating a big commotion as people quickly cleared its path. A man was then pulled out of the ambulance and onto a stretcher. His head was bleeding, and the skin all over his skull was dangling, and could have come off easily from his body with a gentle touch. I turned back in disgust only to come face to face with a pale old man whose eyes were leaking blood, being carried through the corridor by one of the hospital staff. I failed to have a control over myself and the next thing I know, I was a spewing tank of water, vomiting all over the place. People gathered around me and somebody held me by my shoulders asking me to walk in for medical attention. But I pushed the person and darted to the parking lot.

The sight of blood and the bleeding eye had scared the living daylights out of me. The magnitude of misery was vicious here. I felt as if I was condemned to the most barbarous retribution. I rode back to the flat as quick as possible. My efforts to get rid of those terrible images were unsuccessful and those horrific visuals kept surfacing ceaselessly before my eyes, leaving my body shivering. By the time it was dusk, my body had completely heated up with fever.

Edwin, after a long day, entered the house and was surprised to see me curled up on my bed, burning with fever. He gave me some medicine, asking me repeatedly what was wrong. I, however, was too energy-less to utter even a single word of what had happened to me.

It was in the middle of the night when I got up to have some water that I realized Ed was not in his bed. I went inside the washroom and noticed that he was softly talking to himself in the mirror.

"Who the hell are you talking to?" I asked

"Practicing for an audition tomorrow. And by the way, why were you so flummoxed?"

"Let's walk to the terrace," I said. "I am in need of some fresh air."

The flurry of air restored my mental balance. I told him the entire story. He silently commiserated and asked me to forget it like a bad dream.

"I will not return to that work again," I announced

"It's perfectly okay, Charlie," he said, "You can find another job."

After few minutes of peace, we plunged into speaking about how contrasting the atmosphere of our small village was to this illustrious city of Etiole.

The memories of our life left behind – the small room, the orphanage where we had spent our childhood, where we stayed till turning sixteen, and the humble bakery where we used to work – were all lucid and vivid in our minds. Maybe the place where you come from always stays with you, no matter how good or bad it is. You unconsciously learn to live with it and love it too.

Ed then turned the subject of our talk to his moments spent with the love of his life – Claire. Never did he let a day pass without seeing her. But now, he had no idea when they'd meet again. He was sad about it. Extremely depressed rather. Nevertheless, he said that it was like an investment for the coming years of his life. Without moving away from her, as he couldn't have had a better life with her.

The next morning my flat-buddies were surprised to see me not getting ready for work. Ed thankfully took on the task of telling everybody the experience I had had in the hospital and how it had ended up jolting me.

Max believed that working as some waiter or any other odd job would not help me make enough money and would rather call for a lot of hard work. Therefore, he advised me to return to the job without giving it a second thought.

"I know a few people who went from sales to odd jobs but now regret their decision. So I don't want you to quit it over a small thing and regret later on. These odd jobs will only consume a hell lot of your time, even your weekends."

Though I couldn't help agreeing with him, I was not willing to go back to that place and feel miserable again. Hence, to finally convince me, the guys suggested the only way to face hospitals was to get drunk. It did not sound too bad to go back with me being only partially conscious to the conditions there. Benoit came with a bottle of liquor, keeping it in front of me and ordering me to drink it.

I was supposed to stop after a few pegs. However, I could not abstain. My friends, one by one, left for work but I kept on drinking and finally got up to get ready for work. My inner voice kept screaming at me that it wasn't right to show up completely drunk, but by now, I had lost control over myself and I picked up my bag and somehow reached the hospital.

Seeing the sway in my steps and the way I was climbing stairs holding the railing, a nurse called in the security. In my highly inebriated state, I believe, I must have thrown a tantrum of the highest order since they dragged me out, slapped me, punched me and tossed me repeatedly until I stopped resisting. Every time I tried to be steady on my feet, I kept falling down and squealing in pain. When I finally gave up, a hand came offering me support. Touched by the benevolence, I looked up and slowly realized that it was the same girl who was in Chaste City a couple of nights back.

She helped me get to my feet. I had bruises all over my face and body, and blood was trickling down from my head and nose. This was definitely not the way I had imagined meeting her again.

"Bring him in," she enjoined, handing me over to the guards.

"But he is drunk and will cause trouble." It was one of the guards who was part of the gang that had beaten me up.

"He is injured and needs medical attention."

They reluctantly dragged me to the examination room and helped me sit on a bed. While the girl started with the first aid, my eyes had gone heavy and I had completely blacked out. After what seemed like days, I opened my eyes and found myself in a common room among many other patients. On the bed next to mine, a father was feeding his son. He was pouring milk into a pipe which went directly through the nose and inside the body of the kid.

It horrified me. What the hell was happening? He was merely a kid of two or three and under enormous pain. I closed my eyes and the scenes I had witnessed the other day flashed before my eyes as well.

Horrified that the sights that may follow can be even more muddling, I locked my mind, stationed my eyes on the floor, stepped out of my bed, and briskly started for the exit door. I promised myself that no matter what, I was not going to stay in there for another minute. But to make this a challenge, a member of the staff saw me trying to escape and shouted at me to stop. I responded with an accelerated speed. Just as I reached the end of the corridor, the guards caught me and began to drag me back.

"Not inside! No! No!" I cried in panic, begging them to stop. But they did not bother. My cries got louder and louder. People stopped to stare at the ruckus I was creating, and the patients equally interested, were peeping out of the doors and windows of their rooms.

The guards tossed me on a bed and stood barricading me until a female voice asked them to leave. I glanced and it was the very same girl once again.

"Why would somebody come to a hospital completely drunk?" she asked, her arms folded.

I sat upright, pulling my sweater down to cover my bare stomach.

"Either there is something really wrong with your mind or something with your life. A normal person would never do such a thing," she said.

How do you answer that, you idiot, I asked myself.

"Will you please speak up, Mister?" she said, clearly irked at my silence.

"Yesterday was my first day at work. I came here to sell medicines." My voice came out low because of the pain. "The first sight I saw was a man whose eyes were bleeding and then there was this person who had his flesh hanging out of his body like it was some withering leaf on a tree. It appalled me so badly that my body kept shivering the whole day. I couldn't stand watching all those horrific scenes, but I had to do my job as I could not afford losing it. So I returned drunk today, thinking that I would be able to do my work and ignore such sights."

"Is that really the truth?"

"Incurably so," I nodded

"Oh God!" she exclaimed with a wide smile on her face, as if it was the sweetest thing she had ever heard.

"I don't know. I cannot see people in such situations. Such suffering, such pain. It's something I cannot handle, to be honest," I said.

"It's perfectly okay," she consoled me coming closer.

A brief silence followed.

"Doctor, I hope you won't object, if I leave now?"

"Of course you are good to go. I will write down some medicines. Make sure you take them. And by the way, I am not a doctor, just a medical intern for now."

"A medical intern who will be a doctor soon, right?"

"Yes! Within a few months."

"You will be a great one."

She smiled and I couldn't stop myself from staring at her like an idiot. That night at Chaste City I could only catch glimpses of her, but right now, watching her standing in front of me was making me feel things that I had never felt before.

"So, will you be back tomorrow? As a part of your job and not as a patient," she asked, shaking my hand.

"I don't think so. I'll have to look for some other job."

"Don't give up on your job."

"If I am unable to sell these medicines, which I am sure I won't be able to, they'll throw me out anyway."

"Well…Can you meet me tomorrow?" she asked me as I took a half step out, and before I knew my mouth had already blurted out my heart, "I want to meet you every day."

She was startled by what I said. I wanted to bash my head on the nearest wall or run as fast as I could.

"What? Why would you want to meet me every day?" she asked while staring at me with a frown on her pretty face.

I tried to make up for my slip up the best possible way I could think of.

"No…no... I said that every day I…I will have to sell medicines every day and everyday seeing all this stuff will spoil my every day and since my every day will be bad, how can I afford my every day to be a bad day?"

"Okay, I got it!"

She controlled her laughter. "Listen, I understand and I do have a solution. Please come to the hospital tomorrow."

"What?" I was shocked.

"No, I mean, please meet me outside Entrance 1 of the hospital."

"But I am not coming inside. No way that is ever happening again."

"You certainly won't have to, I promise."

I was ecstatic. Right on top of the world, wanting to scream my voice out to make everyone feel the intensity of happiness I was feeling at that moment. I saw her then and I was going to see her again. And if lucky, then again and again. She was awesome! Truly awesome! There were no words with which I could describe that indescribable sense of achievement. Not a single one.

♦

"What the hell has happened to you"? Max asked as he opened the door.

"My face has inflated with ecstasy."

"Then why not completely? Why only half of your face?"

"Thank you for your advice, you dolt. This is all because of you," I said in a dramatic tone with a prompt change in my expression.

I, leaving him in confusion, walked inside and called everybody into the hall, and instantly requested everybody to listen to me as I narrated the sequence of events I had gone through, and how it ultimately ended up being the most thankful day in history of my personal existence.

Listening to my joy was a treat for them; at the same time, they were concerned seeing the injuries I had sustained. My face was swollen. I had a bandage under my eye, two on my forehead and on both my elbows as well. I asked them to forget about my injuries and told them that they didn't really hurt. They were minor, I said again and again, and would heal much sooner than expected.

The girl held her promise. She met me in her uniform, looking a bit tired, strands of hair falling out of the ponytail and fatigue reflecting on her face vividly. It was obvious that she had been up all night working and I felt guilty making her work for me as well.

"I am extremely sorry to trouble you," I said as I walked up to her. "You look exhausted."

"It's alright. In fact, this is what I love about my job the most. Being up for anyone at any moment they need you."

"Our world would have been such a better place if we had more people like you."

"Perhaps all of us are good in some way or the other and it's just that we have to decide which part of us we choose to put more in all our actions. That determines the kind of person one is," she said sweetly.

"How are you feeling now? I hope you are doing better," she asked while taking the bag of medicines from me.

"Yeah, I am all good. Couldn't sleep last night though."

"You couldn't sleep because of the pain?" she asked with sudden concern on her face

"No, because I was sleeping the whole day yesterday."

She laughed. "For a guy who is so sensitive to a hospital, you sure can be funny."

"I don't know," I mumbled lost in her words, in her smile and in the beauty of that time.

We then took to the task we had met for. She went inside with the bag of merchandise and left it to me to either follow her or patiently wait for her. I was, of course, going to do the latter. Then after exactly thirty minutes, she returned. I was amazed to see the volume of transactions on my receipt book. It was supremely encouraging. I was going be the next best big thing in the organization if the trend continued, I thought.

"How did you manage to get me such a big number?" I quizzed, surprised and shocked.

"Don't forget, it's my workplace. They all know me very well and will listen to my request any day."

"Incredible!" I was overjoyed.

She asked me to turn up every alternate day wherein she would do the selling for me. I was feeling a bit embarrassed for taking her help almost every day, nevertheless my greed of seeing her didn't need any arguments.

Over the next forty-one days, we met frequently and followed the same routine. She would be waiting at the entrance and would take the merchandise from me and return with a huge sale figure each time. Not once was she late, and was always polite and kind to me, no matter how selfish I appeared for shamelessly getting my work done, and doing nothing in return for her. Not even talking much to her. But it wasn't like I was afraid to initiate anything beyond the basic pleasantries or too shy to strike a conversation, or was being strategic to impress her. It was basically the manner in which her smile made her twinkling eyes look so pretty that each time I looked into them, I was left scouting for words. Her sophistication mingled with her selflessness was her most priceless possession. I always wondered why she was helping me when she barely knew me, but then, isn't this what a wonderful human being is all about?

My targets now were a small figure compared to the sales I had done. Not only had she assisted me with sales in the hospital where she worked, but had also used her contacts in other hospitals of the city to help me further. As a result of all her kindness, I was put among the on-roll workforce of the company, and thus had job security that made my life easier.

It was a lazy Saturday afternoon and we were all discussing about how to spend the weekend and celebrating the fact that I had been made a permanent employee when the twins barged into the room yelling and jumping wildly all over the place and roaring.

"Yes, We got it! We got it!"

We looked at each other, puzzled.

"What are you two talking about?" Ed asked, pulling them apart.

"We have got tickets for tomorrow's football match," Eugene answered, kissing the red glossy sheet in his hand.

"Really?" Our eyes lit up.

"But where the hell did you get them from? The tickets were sold out like a month ago," Jonathan asked, unable to hide his excitement.

"We stole them!" they said in unison with a sense of pride.

"From where?" Max asked. The joy in his voice overpowered his interrogation.

"All you need to know is that you must reach the stadium by six tomorrow, and that's it."

But unfortunately, on the day of the match, I was called to the office to address an urgency. Our regional sales manager had all of a sudden decided to pay a surprise visit to the office as sales in a few territories under the charge of the area manager had seen a heavy downslide. All of us, salesmen, had to listen to whatever new ideas and rules the boss had crafted for us. The meeting had taken almost all of the day and by the time I was out of the office, I was already fifteen minutes late for the match. Making things worse, all means of public transport were prohibited from taking the route to the venue due to security reasons. I ran fast through the boulevards as it was already seven and I was still miles away from the stadium.

However, half way through my plans took a totally different shape. I noticed the girl – the medical intern – walking out from the city library just a few meters ahead of me. I slowed my speed and began to walk towards her. She saw me coming, and stopped as well, tucking hair behind her ears.

"Doctors love reading, is that why you are here?" I asked, smiling.

"Not each one of them, to be honest. But I certainly do. I fall in love with each book that I read." Her voice was heavy and her eyes red.

"Maybe you've luckily only grabbed good books till date."

"Or maybe I am a reader who can be easily impressed."

"Must be every author's dream readership," I said, observing her carefully.

There was this moment of silence then. She was trying to steal her eyes from me as much possible.

"Can I ask you something, if you don't mind?" I asked.

"Yeah, please."

"It appears to me as if you have been crying. Is everything alright?"

She smiled nodding her head. It wasn't convincing at all. Not even by an ounce. She was certainly upset about something.

"And what are you doing here? I never saw you near this library before," she asked.

"Oh! I was going for the match," I said.

"Please go ahead. It was nice meeting you here. I will see you tomorrow at the hospital."

"The match can wait," I said, looking deep into her eyes. "But what's bothering you?"

"Nothing, honestly."

"Look, I won't be able to enjoy the game if I keep wondering what's upsetting you."

"It is nothing, really," she emphasized.

"See, this is now about the huge amount of money I have invested in buying my tickets for the match. During the entire game, I'll keep wondering what's bothering the girl who has helped me out so much, and thus I'll be mentally stressed, unable to cheer for my club. Loss to so many parties, you see."

She didn't give me an expected smile. It worried me and I wondered if it was something seriously grave that was bothering her.

But a few seconds later, she finally broke her silence, "Promise me, you will not share this with anyone."

"You have my word."

"Last week we had a patient admitted in our hospital. He had met with a major accident where a truck hit him from behind. Sadly, he passed away today in the morning. Our senior doctors had ordered us not to let the family know about this. They wanted them to pay the bills for the coming week before informing them. But one of the nurses went to the family and said that she could save their money if they were ready to share half of the saved amount with her. They agreed and she disclosed the news of the patient's death right away and asked for her share of the saved amount the very next moment."

"Oh my God! That is...that is inhumane."

"Yes and I am part of this inhumanity."

"You are just an intern? It was not up to you to choose or decide anyway."

I could see that her eyes were moist and tears were fighting to break out.

"I am studying medicine for a reason. And that is to heal people...not making money or being selfish like I was today."

"Your very thinking proves you aren't at fault, at all."

"I don't know. It's just that..." She seemed to be lost in a battle of words.

"Hey, don't think too much about it. The more you do, the more you'll keep blaming yourself. In fact, let's go for a walk or maybe we can sit somewhere and talk," I said.

"Weren't you heading for the match?"

"It's the quarterfinals today, and it was my friends who had persuaded me to accompany them," I lied very confidently, as if football was the last thing I would ever watch. "I've got tickets for the finals too. I'll enjoy the game then," I said.

"Are you sure?"

"Positive."

"But a few moments ago you were talking about the huge sum of money invested, of some loss to certain parties, and so on. What was that about?"

"Oh! That was all crap," I said. "My friends bought the ticket for me."

"Alright," she said, laughing. "By the way, you don't talk much, do you?"

"What makes you think so?" I asked turning to the opposite side, beginning to walk along with her.

"It's been approximately two months since we have known each other and you never talked much or even asked me my name."

"I could probably say the same for you," I said, half laughing.

She chuckled, extending hand with a smile illuminating her face. "I am Aster Elise Rembert."

"I am Charlie," I replied, shaking hands with her.

"I know," she said. "Saw it on your ID when you were admitted."

"So you slipped your hands in my pockets, huh?"

"Only to fill your form," she answered. "Not to steal your dollars."

"You must have heard it like a million times, yet I hope you won't mind if I tell you that you look unexplainably lovely in black."

"Thank you so much," she said. "You are looking nice as well."

"You don't have to say that in return, it's fine."

"No, I mean it, I swear."

"Really?"

"Yes, of course."

"I am not used to praises. It's that rare eureka moment whenever I hear one."

"Now I will make sure to heap praises on you so much that you'll get strongly addicted to them," she said and laughed, making me laugh along with her.

Aster and I settled ourselves on a bench in the corner of a park close to the library. It was a nice evening to be out, but perhaps the match had attracted most of the people in Etiole. There were barely any people around and we were completely lost in our world.

I was enjoying our conversation and wanted it to go on and on. I prayed to every force out there to stop time even if it had to be in return for a good chunk of my life. How badly I wished that these moments that I was getting with her didn't have to end. Ever.

Laughing and fooling around, soon our confabulation, unfortunately, returned to where it all began. I tried my best to convince her that she had no say or control over it, and yet she wasn't able to get over it, no matter how hard I tried. All this while, I was insanely fighting to control my hands that wanted to wipe the messed kohl under her eyes. Although to me, she was still looking marvelously beautiful. I wondered if she would ever see herself the way I did.

A quarter mile away from the park was a police station and as we were coming back from the park, up ahead on the road, we noticed a few cops dragging five men out of their van. All of them, I could clearly see, were wearing yellow knickers which were too short to be even called knickers and had flags painted from their forehead to their waist lines. The cops dragged them inside while all of them had their hands cuffed. One of them saw me and called my name.

"Ed?" I was surprised recognizing my best friend's voice.

"Do you know them?" Aster asked.

"They are my friends, I guess," I said, confused and stunned.

The cops held them by their necks and carried them inside the station.

Both of us followed quickly.

"So good to see you." An old obese cop, sitting at the end of entrance corridor said looking in my direction. I got further confused.

"Good to see you too, Mr Perks," Aster responded, quickly marching towards him, and that was when I realized that the cop was talking to Aster.

"What are you doing here?" he asked.

"Sir, why did you arrest these people?"

"These rascals stole someone's match tickets. We got a complaint filed against them yesterday."

"Oh!" Aster stood quietly for a few seconds. "Sir, they are my friends. Can you please spare them with a warning today? I promise you'll never see them involved in any crime ever again."

"What? You want me to let these criminals walk away?"

"Sir, I am just trying to protect my friends, that's all. And they are not criminals. They surely aren't."

"I don't believe you could be friends with such people."

"But they are. And they aren't bad, trust me."

The cop now seemed more shocked than me.

"Sir, I request you to let them go, please," Aster requested again.

"Yes sir. Please let us go," Right, sounding more like a wounded puppy, put in his part for a humble request.

"You shut up, bloody criminal!" the cop yelled back.

The cop took a serious look at me and Aster standing in front of him and then at my friends pondering over what exactly was the right thing to do.

"Well, doctor, you had been a savior and guardian angel while I was admitted in the hospital, so it feels cruel to say no to you. So if you know these crackpots, I will spare them with a penalty tonight. But next time if they do anything of the sort, I'll make sure they are behind bars for a long-long time."

"I shall be very thankful, and they won't engage in any sort of mischief, I promise you."

The cop walked to the table and began to fill in the paper work while we silently stood watching him finish the procedures of releasing my friends.

"What about the final tickets?" Aster whispered into my ears then. "Shall we return them right away?"

I shook my head with widened eyes, saying loud in my mind, "I lied. I am sorry. I have none. No final tickets."

She was smart enough to figure everything as she covered her mouth with her hands to avoid the sound of her chortling filling the place. Meanwhile, Eugene paid the fine and thanked the cops for their mercy. They, however, weren't interested in giving a warm reply. Instead, what followed was a stern warning.

"Dare to repeat this again and you shall have rats running over your crops."

Agreeing and acknowledging to the mistakes in fear, and with a sharp sense of disbelief of escaping what could have been a very bad night, we moved out absolutely dumbstruck. My friends walked behind us with heads bowed in embarrassment, avoiding eye contact.

"Guys, I'll walk Aster to her place and see you in the room," I said a few minutes later.

"No. I am fine. I'll manage. It's not a problem," she said.

"No, please allow me to walk you back to your room. It's the least I can do after what you have done for me and my friends."

"Yes!" Ed jumped in. "We do appreciate what you did for us We just don't know how to show our gratitude. At least let him walk you home safely."

I was honestly overwhelmed by what she had done for Ed and the rest of my friends. And just as Ed said, I had no clue how to show my gratitude to her. First she had helped me with my job without asking for anything in return and now, had helped my friends. The realization that not once had I repaid her benevolence made me cringe inside. I had to work hard to persuade her to let me walk her home and all the way I was occupied by the realization that I was taking advantage of her kind heart.

"Charlie, is everything alright? You seem to be bothered by something."

"I was just thinking how much I owe you for all that you have done for me and my friends."

"You don't owe me anything."

"You are being modest, too modest in fact. All I have been doing is taking help from you over and over again and never once thanking you properly."

"Charlie, stop! You are over thinking."

"Will you at least let me take you out for dinner?"

"I am sorry. I have a tight schedule. Interns have to, at times, work for like sixteen hours a day!"

"I guess I should stop taking any help from you then."

"What?"

"Yeah. Let me lose my job. I mean, you do so much for me and now I feel like I am being totally selfish."

"You don't have to take it that way. Okay fine, pick me up in the evening the coming Saturday at eight?"

"That will be perfect," I said, smiling.

The guys were all over me when I came out wearing my rented suit on Saturday evening. They were checking me heedfully and went over everything from the clothes to my hair to what I would be saying to Aster. I had to keep reminding them that we were not going on an official date but only a casual dinner together. The care and concern they continued to shower made me feel like I was part of a lovely family. All of them came downstairs to escort me to the taxi, doling out advice till the taxi drove off.

I took Aster to the place where I had seen her for the first time: Chaste City. But it was a restaurant this time and not a bar. I told her to order anything she wanted and that dinner was on me as a small token of appreciation for what she had done for all of us.

Over dinner we talked about how I had bumped into her, the lie about the finale tickets, the way she took away the pressure of my sales targets and also the details of how Right-Left were at war with each other since the police arrest. Somehow with Aster I felt at so much ease that I started sharing things with her that I had never done with anybody else except Ed.

"What do you love doing the most, Charlie?" she then asked.

"Writing," I instantly replied.

"That's awesome," she said. "It's such a gift to be able to express yourself that way."

"Not anymore though."

"What? You mean you don't write anymore?"

"Yeah, Kind of."

"Can I ask why?"

"It's a long story."

"I still want to know."

I looked at her half smiling, silently pleading to spare me from narrating and reliving those dark memories but looking at her, I did not have the heart to refuse, I don't know why.

"When I was in high school, I was madly in love with writing, and that's probably the only thing I ever did with utmost dedication. I always used to dream of people reading my books and falling in love with the way I would describe feelings. Every line I used to write was perhaps a piece of my own soul. During the last year of school, there was an inter-state story writing competition and fortunately, my story won the first prize."

"That must have been amazing," she interrupted, very excited.

"Yes, but the name published under my story was that of my teacher. He had stolen it. I complained, but people just made fun of me. No one expected a kid to defeat his master. I created a big fuss in my school and I was thrown out with a blank transfer certificate that put an end to my academic career, and writing as well."

"You gave up writing for that?"

"Life never gave me another chance to write."

"Come on, Charlie! You must accept that you just simply gave up? Yes, I agree what happened with you was ugly, but it wasn't by any means the end of the world."

"You'd probably not understand, Aster as you could never feel that pain because it is mine. It is easy to counsel someone but the exigent part is to be in that person's place and go through a tribulation that completely shatters you."

Observing that her arguments were hardly convincing me, she said, "Okay. I will tell you a small story, that's true. Would you mind listening?"

"Go ahead."

"There was a cute little girl. Everything was perfect about her life. She had the most loving parents, the safest home and everything she wished for. On her thirteenth birthday, her parents met with an accident. Her father died on the spot while her mother was rushed to hospital in a critical state. Two days later she slipped into a coma. The girl looked up to the doctor with hope, expecting him to be that guardian angel, who would wake her mother from that evil sleep. But instead, the doctor exploited the girl's infirmity and began molesting her, terrorized her, and threatened her that if she told anyone, he would kill her mother. She did not want to lose her at any cost. The girl was slapped, pulled by her hair, bitten, punched and thrown around. He would do drugs and make that faultless child do anything he wanted. On some occasions he would insert objects in her body, leaving her soaked in blood. Cigarettes, medical tools and anything in his hand – her flesh bore the brunt of all of them. She cried as he mercilessly scratched her body, hollered in pain, but that man…he was diffused with animalism and bereft of humanity. Once the girl even shaved her eyebrows, presuming that he would find her beastly and leave her alone, but it only turned her into a laughing stock among everyone she came across. God did not respond to her prayers. She would hug her father's picture and beseech him to return each single day. For four years the doctor inflicted his lust on the girl until her mother finally died. Eventually, she left the city, but those terrible years accompanied her forever."

There was silence in the air for the next few minutes.

"Do you know who that girl was, Charlie?" Aster asked, tears rolling down her cheeks.

I nodded my head fearing the inevitable.

"It was me…Aster."

Her words completely froze me, and a shiver ran down my spine. I could see how hard she was trying to hold herself. She kept looking into my eyes with her tear-filled ones. I didn't know what to say or how to console her, as hers was a pain that stood compounded with time.

"If I could decide not to give up, Charlie, you should too. Proclaim your spirit to hold on and withstand the odds. Sign off like a champion. Every single day will give you a new reason to be unhappy, but nature has given us powers within us to overpower all that's negatively affecting us. Writing happens to be that gift of yours, healing happens to be mine. If we'll quit, we will somewhere defeat nature's very purpose of making us."

Unbelievable! She was filled with love for life despite being subjected to the fires of hell. Coerced every single day for four straight years, she managed to bounce back to end up studying medicine.

All my life I had been angry at God, first for depriving me from the warmth and affection of my parents and then for leaving me to struggle for even the basic things like food, sleeping space, education and a job. But today, watching and listening to Aster made me feel really small even for thinking that I had been dealt bad cards in life. In spite of everything that had happened in her life, she was one of the generous and kindest persons I had ever met. Any other with a dark past like hers would have turned spiteful, but not Aster. Not her.

I recalled how magically she had grabbed my attention the very first moment I had seen her, and then over the past few months she had won my respect. But that day, she sincerely took my heart away. That night I could not help the tears flowing from my eyes. I was lying on the mattress, listening to the silence of the night and feeling Aster's mortifying emotion. Her smiling face with infinite agony behind it kept flashing before my eyes the entire night.

I was feeling extremely close to her and terribly broken as if her pain was my own. I didn't know whether it was the heart-wrenching episode that had tied my heart to hers or her persona that conquered my heart and brain altogether, but what I really knew was that I had fallen for her. And I just wanted to be with her and love her until the end of time. What a wonderful girl she was! Through her story, she didn't want sympathy for herself. She wanted to inspire me. She wanted me to accomplish my goals, and in return, she wanted nothing.

How on earth could I let such a girl go?

Two days later when we met again outside the hospital, I could see that Aster had not come empty handed. She was hiding something behind her. I chose not to ask and pretended I hadn't noticed.

"Give me your hand," she said, without responding to my greetings.

As I extended my hand, she placed a beautiful diary in it.

"Open it, please," she requested

I flipped it open and found that she had scribbled something on the first page.

Dear Charlie,

Anyone on this earth can steal what you have written, but no matter how powerful or cunning the person is, they can never rob you of the feelings with which you write. Honestly, I believe all of us come with an inimitable originality that can only be produced by our very own heart and nothing else. Others, well they might succeed to get a piece of your work by unfair means but they will never be able to replicate what makes you 'you' – your uniqueness. Therefore, never stop writing. What is being tricked away from you shall always remain impure and less meaningful unless you are the medium to narrate it to the world.

Bad things don't happen every day, and in case they do, they eventually intend to take you to something phenomenal, something that is extraordinary, beyond the goodness you have imagined or planned for your own future.

I earnestly hope that someday I will have a copy of your book signed by you that I can flaunt, saying that such a great writer happens to be my friend.

Yours,
Aster Elise Rembert.

Suddenly I realized that the most cardinal event of our life is not when our dreams materialize, but when people who mean everything to us, re-kindle our lost desires. That is when distress of failure sets us free, and hopefulness overtakes the result of our earnest endeavors.

Her move touched me. I felt strong enough to prevent myself from crumbling again. I had no idea how many more encounters my destiny was going to fix with her but I was sure that these words of hers were going to carry me through every repugnant phase of life.

"Did you like the gift?" she asked.

"How do I thank you, Aster? This is perhaps the most amazing thing I have ever received in my life."

"If you want to really thank me, give writing a fresh start."

Aster didn't know what her words were doing to me. She made me fall in love with her even more deeply. How badly I wished to tell her what her words and what she had started to mean for me. Overwhelmed by passion and those warmest feelings, I stood silent, unable to convey my feelings.

"Charlie, you'll start writing, right? Promise me!"

What she didn't know was that the moment she had shared her darkest and cruel past to me, I had started seeding the will to start writing again. And now, her encouraging words had made that seed grow powerful roots, never to waver. I didn't have to think twice to make a promise to her.

"I promise I will start writing again."

"Thank you so much," Aster said with such a radiant smile that my mind instantly wove a beautiful picture of a life together with Aster where she held on to me with all the love I could wish for.

"Hey, would you like to join me for breakfast?" Aster brought me back from my reverie and erasing the beautiful dream.

"Sure," I said.

"Let's go to the cafeteria then."

The horrible images of the day when I had first landed in this very hospital rushed into my mind.

"No chance in blue hell!" I half shouted, suddenly thinking about the terrifying scenes I might have to encounter on the way.

"We have a cafeteria behind the building. Patients don't go there, so don't worry."

"Oh! That's fine then," I said.

The cafeteria was an extension of the hospital. The walls and the whole interior imbibed the monochrome colour palette of the entire building.

"How do you survive with such kind of food?" I asked, almost spitting out the bite of the over-salted omelet I had taken.

"They have messed it up today. Otherwise, they are generally good." Having said that, she immediately called the waiter, requesting him to replace my food.

"Can I ask you something, Aster?" I asked as the waiter went away clearing the plates.

"Sure," she said.

"How could you share such a grave thing that happened in your life so easily with me?

She smiled as if she was expecting the question.

"It's never the reason of your pain or its magnitude that determines whether it can be shared or not. It's the compassion and security you feel in someone's company that makes you do so. Moreover, I thought, better than giving you examples of a genius or some special achiever, I should tell you about an ordinary girl who was trying to overcome her dark past."

"No, Aster. You are not ordinary, but extra-extraordinary. Nobody could have done what you did, or be as strong as you have been."

"It's nice to listen to good things about oneself. That hasn't happened to me in years."

"What do you say that? I am sure your family will agree with what I just said."

"I don't have a family," she said, shooting a look towards the counter.

"So you have no one to call a family? Like a brother, a sister, or a cousin maybe?"

"No, I have been on my own for years now."

I felt like such an idiot for asking her about her family and scratching that wound of hers, when I was not alien to the pain of having nobody to call family.

I could very well understand how it felt to be so alone in this world. But what puzzled me much about her was how someone who was in so much pain, could be so loving? Was it her way of living or was it indeed a way of living? Each day that I spent with her was just another reason for me to know her better.

I was observing her continuously: her smile, her eyes, the way she used to flip her hair and tuck the strands behind her ear; the tiny diamond earring she wore that kept playing hide and seek through her hair, could not have looked more beautiful on any other girl in the world. Everything about her was unique to me, absorbing me and drawing me towards her intensely. I loved her, I simply loved her.

"There is a book reading session tomorrow," Aster said as we walked out of the cafeteria after finishing our food. "Would you like to come along?"

"Instead, why not sit in a quiet place and talk to each other."

"Quiet place? That makes you sound like a man with intentions, huh?"

"What if you are their target?"

"What?" Aster asked me baffled and making me realize that I had yet again gone on to prove my idiocy by letting my mouth act before my brain. This was the second time that I had let my feelings for Aster slip out of my mouth.

"I am just kidding. So where is the book reading?" I said trying to gather the situation and change the topic.

"Let's go to a quiet place," Aster said and thankfully didn't pick on my slip of tongue so I was happy to change the topic.

"But you wanted to go to the book reading."

"Maybe I can have you do it for me there and that shall serve both our purposes, isn't it?"

"You are such an expert at coming up with solutions."

"Despite that, I am still so down to earth."

"Yes, indeed," I said, unable to stop laughing. Aster joined me as well. It felt so good to be able to share such moments with her.

"By the way, which novel am I supposed to be bringing along?" I aksed her.

"I shall take care of that."

"Alright, I will see you in the evening then. Take care."

I started to walk away, leaving Aster at the hospital entrance and that's when she stopped me.

"What about the sales?"

"What sales?" I asked confused.

"The medicines," Aster said pointing at my bag of medicines.

"Oh! I almost forgot." I took my bag off and handed it to her.

We were sitting by the lakeside. My reading that had lasted for slightly more than two hours had, according to her, made her day worthwhile. We gazed at the water reflecting the endless evening sky that was filled with twinkling stars. It was unlike Etiole – very peaceful, without many people and without anything to steal our attention.

Aster had brought me a copy of her favourite author for our little reading session, but now she wanted me to read out my own work to her. The day after she had given me the diary, I had battled the entire night to write something. But all I could do was, stare at Aster's beautiful handwriting and those beautiful words she had written for me. So I decided to be honest with her.

"Aster, I have started to write, although I could not specifically decide what to write about. I did get success with a few thoughts initially, but on the whole it appears like my talent has lost its soul or charm or whatever it is. Even after scratching my head for a long time, no extraordinary idea occurred to me. I guess, I am too young to write or haven't lived long enough to write something valuable or something that can create a difference."

Aster shot an angry look at me. Seemingly, she had no regard for my perception.

"You don't have to live enough to write, Charlie," she said. "Rather, you must feel to write. When you sit down the next time and discern that you cannot pen down anything, ask yourself: what is my life all about, and what has managed to touch the deepest extremity of my heart? Most importantly, don't try to make things special. Just keep them true and simple. And then you will realize how incredibly your words will weave magic that will wonderfully impact each person who reads it."

I nodded my head, smiling. Being with Aster was like being shipped onto the shoreline of eternal serenity. No problems could bug me when I was with her. She had a solution to every impediment in my life. What a wonder this girl was turning out to be!

"I am starving," Aster said. "Have you been to the old market of Etiole? I know a great place there."

"Nahh! I thought Etiole only had some old buildings."

"Then let me treat you to the best meal you'll ever taste in Etiole."

"Sure, My highness."

The old market was in complete contrast to the affluent face of the city that I had been accustomed to ever since I had been in Etiole. The streets were put together in odd colour combinations, but that also added to its historical charm. The place was filled with crowds interested in shopping and visibly starving too, as each food joint in the place had a long queue of people waiting to be served.

I joined a long line of people, up for their turn to buy hot chocolate on a stall while Aster stood waiting for me under a decorated tree at the edge of the cobbled street. Someone was playing the bagpipe nearby. However, that did not prevent me from hearing a guy standing on my left

"Check that chick standing under the tree. Man, what a bombshell! Let's walk from behind and when we reach close, push me towards her. I want to grab her butt."

I turned around and to my horror I realized that the guys were headed towards Aster. It dawned on me that they were talking about her. The guys were already drawing close and one of them pushed the other as they had been discussing. But before they could succeed, I rushed to Aster and held her from her waist and got her out of the way. Then as he stretched his hand, I caught it and kicked him right on the face. He fell down, rolling like a ball. I grabbed the guy and sat on him, banging his nose with my head and slapping his face. Aster begged me to stop but I was so mad that I couldn't stop myself from beating up that jerk.

"How dare you to disrespect her, you son of a bitch!" I had blood in my eyes.

Someone hit me from behind with a brutal force, making me fall flat on the ground. A group of people had taken advantage of my vulnerability and started kicking. To my utter surprise, Max, Eugene, Benoit, Jonathan and Ed appeared out of nowhere.

"You can never do it without me," Ed said, dragging two boys away from me.

Our gang was ferocious as a lion and pounced on those douche bags with all savagery – raining punches on their faces, and kicks in their ribs, and endless slaps on the backs of their heads. In a few minutes they had their lessons learnt.

Finishing off with what they had started, I went to Aster who seemed livid with anger.

"I can explain," I said.

"How can you explain what just happened, Charlie?"

"Look! This guy…he was…"

I didn't know how to tell her what their intention was.

"He was disrespectful to you. And any man who talks ill about you is going to get ripped apart."

"So you are going to beat them like an animal?"

"I can be worse if it's about hurting you."

"But you don't have to do something that hurts you in any way. That makes no sense."

"Don't worry, I will be fine. I have this friend, who happens to be a doctor. She will take care of me if anything happens to me."

She almost laughed, but then contained herself, biting her lip to show that she still didn't approve of what had just happened.

"She will take care of me, won't she?" I said.

She looked into my eyes, nodding her head with a big goofy smile.

◆

Though Aster had let me off easily, Max had no intention to do the same. Max and I were sitting on the terrace and drinking beer and he was furious at the way I had behaved.

"Why did you get into a brawl in a place where you almost know no one? Do you have the faintest idea what fights in Etiole can turn into?" Max had been constantly explaining the ways in which this fight could have gone wrong if they hadn't showed up at the right time.

"They wanted to harass Aster. How could I let that happen?" I asked angrily, unable to make Max understand why I had to do it.

"It's not important to address everything, mate. You could have ignored them and taken her away."

"Making her feel safe is much more important for me than acting mature, Max."

"How exactly do you make her feel safe by breaking into a fight?"

"By making her know that no matter what goes wrong, there is someone in the world who'll be there for her. Orphans don't get that privilege often, Max. Our lives are spent constantly searching for a roof above our heads."

"Will you take bullets to your heart for her?"

"I'll prefer to take them in my head. My heart is reserved for her."

"It's tough to argue with a man who has fallen in love," he said, laughing. "So, have you told her yet that you love her?"

"No. Not yet."

"Waiting for the right time?"

"I guess so."

"Don't wait for a right time, buddy. If you are sure, make this the right time."

"Her past discourages me to express my feelings to her. I am afraid that she may feel that my love is but sympathy for her. Or some sort of kindness."

The night when Aster had shared her past with me, it had stirred me in more ways than I had imagined. At one end, I had the greatest respect and on the other end I had this huge revelation that Aster was the one for me. But the fear of how I could confess my love to a girl who had such great pain hidden inside her had made me go crazy and hit the bottle that night. I had poured out my heart to Max about Aster's past. He was kind enough to not question me further or mention it again. I was cursing myself for letting it out and breaking her trust in some way.

"I am sorry. I don't think she'll feel that way. See, the reality is, people mock at girls who have been raped. Sympathy is not shown to lessen her pain, but to quench this insatiable spirit of enquiry. Consequently, a girl first suffers at the hand of a rapist then by the questions of the society. Now in between all of this, if you go and tell her that you want to live with her, you'll send a message directly to her heart, that she hasn't been rendered untouchable by being raped and that she is as normal as any other girl."

"You are right, Max. She committed no mistake."

"No matter how strong, she badly needs someone to tell her this."

"So I should do it?"

"Of course," he said, tossing the empty bottle into a corner. "Any delay might lead to regret."

A few beer bottles later he left to sleep while I...I kept looking at the city, thinking whether I should really go ahead and tell Aster everything and jeopardize what we had now. I had no doubt in my mind about my love for her, but I had a fear that she wouldn't love me back. Maybe it was sort of an expectation which had all the power to hurt me in the end if not fulfilled, but then there was no other way of living my life with her. The first time I had seen her, she was simply a treat to me, but now, she was all that I needed for the rest of my fated time.

It was an overcast evening, with the scent of spring blowing all around, and making everything sway benignly to its tunes. Aster and I were sitting in the society park close to her hospital. There were countless people, jogging on the pathways bordered by trees on both sides. Seemingly, they had decided to go an extra mile before the heat of the summer would force them to stay inside their homes. I drew my attention on confessing my feelings to Aster. I noticed how overtly she was amused by a group of children, who in their freedom of innocence were going round and round our bench, cackling and pushing each other for the ball.

"When we were kids, we wanted to quickly grow up, and now when we are adults, we wish to be kids again," Aster said as she zipped her jacket to protect herself from the gentle breeze.

"I wish I too had that sort of a childhood," I said.

"Why do you say that?"

"Not all of us are lucky, Aster. Not each one of us is given the same set of things."

"What's the matter?"

'I must have been two or three months old when my parents left me outside the door of an orphanage with a note hooked to my shirt. If I go back to my childhood, the first memories that flash before my eyes are of being battered by a teenage boy. He wanted to snatch my chocolates that some rich kid had distrubuted on his birthday. It was then that Edwin came to my rescue and we became best friends thereafter. The sort of life and encounters that held our hands were either forgettable or highly regrettable. There were many consecutive days, I can recall, which would pass without any food. We used to sometimes steal, get caught and then mistreated in all ways you can imagine. And then, when we turned sixteen, we moved out of that dungeon and rented a room in the most infamous part of our village. The room we lived in had a broken roof and we never had enough money to get it repaired for all the seven years that we stayed in there. Then, a few months back, we moved to Etiole because Edwin wanted to try his hands at acting. I accompanied him, because he is all I have and not because I expected any transformation in my own personal life. After suffering from depression when my story was stolen and my academic career came to an end, I kept myself away from most of the things I wished to experience. But you Aster – your company, your words, and each and everything about you – pushes me to find the lost boy in myself who wants to do something good with his life. Your concern may be a regular part of who you are, but for me, you are no less than a life saver. Thank you, Aster. Thank you so much for being my friend."

I stopped just in time to stop my mouth from saying, 'I love you'.

Aster kept looking into my eyes with a wide smile, and then slapped me gently saying, "Don't thank me. Just make sure to have my name right there on top of the acknowledgement page of your book."

"That goes without saying. But I hope that your boyfriend doesn't take it otherwise. About your role, you know."

"I have no boyfriend." She laughed. I was glad that she didn't see the evil smile on my face.

"That's a lie. That is the hardest thing to believe," I said mentally thanking all the Gods for keeping Aster single.

"I don't, honestly," Aster said with a shrug.

"There must be someone still, whom you, I mean want to be with or love."

"No. The weight of my past does not let me love anyone, Charlie," she replied. "I don't have feelings left in me anymore. It's over. The love in me is gone now."

Those words were like a bolt of electricity to my heart as she had just voiced my greatest fear. I had feared that Aster may be reluctant to trust another person after what had happened to her and she confirmed that.

"But you have to get over what that doctor did to you," I said.

"What's the point of getting over something when people push you back to it again and again?" Aster had tears in her eyes.

"Hey, what happened?"

"Nothing," she said, wiping her tears.

I got on my knees, holding her hand and said, "Tell me Aster, what happened?"

"Nothing, Charlie."

"Please, Aster. I request you."

Tears still dropping from her eyes, she said, "When I came to Etiole and entered school, a guy said that he loved me. I was still hiding in the shadows of my past, becoming much of a recluse as the days turned into weeks and weeks turned into months. But honestly, somewhere inside, I always wanted someone to come to me and make me feel really wanted. This guy, he did every single thing possible to bring a smile on my face. Then I told him everything about my past, and all of a sudden, he felt disgusted to have fallen for a rape victim. For a girl who had been rendered filthy because a beast unleashed himself on her for four years. He said that I was impure and my past would bring disgrace to his blue-blooded family. So I left making a pact to never fall for anyone ever again, because ultimately, what everyone craves for in love is your body and not your soul."

Piercing through the silence that followed, she continued, "You know, it's tough to survive without love, without anyone telling you that you mean the world to them, and that you really do matter. But then, what hurts you even more is when you learn that the person who once cared for you, is humiliated by who you really are. You feel like you should have never met them and you wish you could go back in time and erase them out of your brain, out of your memories, out of your heart and start everything all over again."

"Do you still love him?" I asked.

"Not at all."

"Then move on, Aster. Forget what happened to you."

"If you were in my place, Charlie, would you have been able to do that?"

"I don't know." I paused for a moment, thinking "May be, I guess, you are right."

I was so glad that I had stopped myself from blurting out my feelings. Had it happened, I would have ruined everything. Clearly, Aster feared to entrust her feelings and affections with another person, and rightfully so. Now after learning more about her, I wasn't even sure that I was the person who could help her erase every dark chapter in her life. Maybe it was the right decision to not confess my feelings. Maybe this was the length of my time with Aster. My heart lay pierced, stabbed, battered and bruised and I had no more courage to face Aster.

"I think it is better that I leave now. I have some office work to complete."

I left the place, wishing every second that she'd stop me and run to me to say that she loved me. But neither did she call me back, nor did I stop and it further convinced me that maybe Aster would never reciprocate my feelings. I was tugging on to a false hope that she would accept me after all.

My life, in a moment's time, had returned back to that similar road where there was aimless movement but no meaningful halt. That revitalizing sensation of seeing her again and dreaming to have a family with her had suddenly vanished. I felt like I had lost something very significant, something that had been a part of me since ages. I refused to eat anything that night. I wished I had met Aster in her childhood, or maybe had killed that doctor when he tried to touch her. Or I should have moved to Etiole and met her before that jerk broke her heart.

I was spiraling down with a sense of deprival, shutting myself in the only room in the house and avoided talking to the guys or answering their questions or the banging on the door when Eugene came yelling to the door of the room.

"Charlie, someone's there for you."

I didn't bother to reply or even acknowledge his presence. He knocked the door hardest. I still was unmoved.

"Charlie, douche bag. Someone's there for you." He was clearly running out of patience.

"Leave me alone, Eugene. I don't want to see anyone," I shouted.

"Charlie?"

It was Aster's voice. I slapped myself to make sure I wasn't hearing voices.

I rushed towards the door wearing my pajamas just to make sure that I hadn't gone crazy.

"What are you doing here?" I asked, totally surprised.

"You left your order book with me. I thought you would need it."

"Oh yeah. Thank you." I faked a smile, taking the diary from her and finding the tiny sliver of hope melting away.

"Okay then. I will take my leave. Take care."

"You too."

She stood there, her eyes wandering aimlessly, but absolutely refusing to look at mine.

"Can you just come out for a minute please?" she asked, hesitatingly.

"Sure."

She turned and I followed her through the dark, cold corridor. It was pitch dark there as always and I could feel Aster's hand on mine seeking guidance through the corridor. She held on to my hand tight and did not let the grip loosen until we stopped at the exit gate with the golden street light shining right above our heads.

"You lied to me," she said, angrily.

"Lied to you? Lied about what?"

"You said you weren't able to write anything."

"Yeah. I wasn't."

"Then what is this paper all about?" she asked, taking one out from her hand bag.

"What paper?" I reached for the paper but she moved my hand away and unfolded it to read it out to me.

Dear Aster,

One fine morning, I will get up to notice my face in wrinkles and furrows. My hair will be scattered all over the pillow; most of them will be grey without a doubt. The spring of youth will have made way for my final years, and I'll no longer be able to walk swiftly. My voice will tremble as a result of impairment; it will get hard for me to read words and things will get no better until I close my eyes forever.

I'll spend every minute terrorized, unwilling to end this beautiful journey of being in this world. However, I'll cheerfully accept this truth of life, if you hold my hand, and promise to walk with me, until we breathe. Because no matter how ugly both of us look seventy years or a million years from now, I'll take you in my arms with the same devotion that I'll do it for the very first time.

Charlie.

I kept looking at her while she clutched the papers tightly in her trembling hands with tears rolling down her eyes.

"You would never leave me, right?" she asked looking deeper into my eyes.

"If you'll want me to stay, I won't ever leave," I said.

"So my past doesn't bother you in any way?"

"All I know is that you are the strongest girl I have ever met. I love you, not for how beautiful your body is, but how astonishingly you overcame every difficulty life threw at you. Moreover, whenever I am with you, I feel like what I would certainly have been if I was not an orphan. And I won't say I will die if you won't love me back, but not a single minute of my life will pass without thinking how wonderful life would have been in your presence."

"Then why did you leave me in that park alone?"

"I was...I was just so numb." I looked at her in the eyes now sparkling with tears of affection. "But to be honest, I wanted you to stop me."

"And I kind of wanted you to stay there and tell me that you won't ever leave me."

"I lost hope when you said you won't love anyone ever."

"When a person has fallen down and they say that they fear to get up, they don't necessarily mean it. They might just mean that they want the most loving hand to defeat their fear."

"I guess...I guess that's why I held your hand when I was lying drunk in the hospital."

She laughed through her tears as both of us stood motionless, gauging the depth of that unsaid pain in each other's eyes.

"I love you, Aster."

"And I love you."

Her words made me feel like I had just conquered every precious thing in the world. I smiled, tucking a strand of her hair behind her ear and placed her head on my chest softly. Then as she looked into my eyes, I kissed her forehead saying, "I want to spend every minute of my life with you."

She smiled moving up, standing on toes and softly letting her lips touch mine, and ran her hands through my hair. I could feel the warmth of her soft fingers. They were so delicate. It was a moment that was going to last till eternity.

Nothing in this world is more amazing than the feeling of being loved. I was on cloud nine, sheathed with the sugary memories of the previous night when Aster had reciprocated my feelings for her. I was rejoicing and still couldn't digest the fact that Aster loved me as well. It was such an amazing feeling to know that whenever I will slow down in life, a loved one will be standing right by my side with everything imperative to take me ahead.

"People lose heart in love but this man seems to have lost his mind too. Look at him! His eyes aren't blinking and his smile isn't leaving his face," Ed told Jonathan, watching me sitting lost on my bed with an abiding smile on my face.

It was the first relationship of my life. I was naturally sanctioned to cut off myself from the world for a few days. I mean, it made sense to wallow in fantasizing my coming days with my girl, holding her tight in my arms, dancing with her in the rain, and kissing her under the blue sky.

"The kid isn't used to handling girls. Let him enjoy the frenzy for a few days. Afterwards, that smile will be a rare thing," Jonathan remarked, giggling.

"Charlie, there is a phone call for you," Max handed me the phone with a smirk on his face.

"Is it from my office?" I asked.

He wouldn't answer.

"Hello?"

"Hi, Charlie. It's me, Aster."

Now I knew why Max had that smirk on his face and why he wouldn't say who was on the phone. I also happened to notice that suddenly all the guys were standing way too close to me. I waited for them to leave but it was obvious that I was not going to get any privacy. They didn't even bother about the glares I was giving them or all the silent pleading to leave me alone. There was no other option but to talk to Aster in front of the guys.

"Hey Aster, How are you?" I finally said.

"I am alright. But are you...? You sound a little...off! Everything alright?"

How could I possibly tell her that I was surrounded by prying eyes and ears and that I couldn't talk to her comfortably?

"Yeah! Everything is alright."

"No, it's not.... Let me guess! Your friends are around you, aren't they?"

I couldn't stop myself from laughing out loud. The guys were taken aback for a minute. It was amazing how Aster knew me so well.

"Yes, they are," I said in between. My unstoppable laughter made her laugh too. It was so good to hear that full of life laugh echoing in my ears.

"Alright. I will keep it short and leave you to be tortured by the guys then. Will you please reach Gate Six of Matrix Grand Arena by seven tonight?"

"Sure. Anything serious?"

"No. Nothing serious. I thought we could go to the concert together, if it is alright with you?"

"I would love to. Will meet you there at seven."

"Great. See you in the evening then, Charlie."

"Alright," I said as I hung up the phone.

"Are the kids leaving for their honeymoon?" Ed asked, giggling.

"We are just going to a concert, you dumbass," I shouted while throwing an apple at him with full force.

♦

Matrix Grand Arena was jam packed with people. The waiting line was so long that it considerably stretched out of the Arena. One of the living legends Albert Ferguson was performing that night and the excitement among the people was absolutely intoxicating. It took me ages to locate Aster in the maddening crowd and the colossal queue of people.

We got into the stadium in much lesser time than we had expected. The stage was thundering with the sounds of guitars. The crowd was going bonkers, craving for more and more. Everyone present was dying to see Albert Ferguson – a legendary artist who was no less famous for his looks as much as he was for his music. His versatile singing would make you fall in love with him.

The lights were dimmed all of a sudden, and promptly a spot light appeared on the stage. Thirty thousand people were chanting his name without a pause as he entered from the back to take the center stage.

As he grabbed the microphone, people intensified their chants and did not even let him speak. He was enjoying the love of the thousands of people who had gathered just to see him live in action. The expression on his face said it all. Albert moved on to the ramp, waving his hands to show gratitude for the overwhelming love of the fans.

The fans were on the zenith of craziness which made me think how awesome it would be to watch Edwin one day. 'The life of a man!' as he loved to call it. There would be a time when he would witness the same level of restlessness among the masses just for a glimpse of him. He would be a star one day and I was sure of it. Very sure.

We were almost in the last row of the crowd and had it not been for the huge screens installed around, it would have been impossible to watch Albert croon his popular songs. With each song people were growing more and more euphoric. It was around his fourth or fifth song that my attention was suddenly drawn to Aster. She was howling in pain. The person standing in front of us had accidently banged his head on Aster's nose while head banging.

"Hey, are you fine?" I asked, checking on her.

Aster shook her head, unable to understand what I was saying. She was checking if her nose was bleeding. Luckily, it wasn't. It had bruised a bit though.

"Aster, are you alright?" The volume of the music was sky touching and we could barely hear each other.

"Yeah. Just a little accident!"

Though she said it was a minor bump, I could see that her nose was all red and if that was not enough, the guy had started with his fierce head banging again. I moved to teach the guy how to behave in a crowd and stop with his head banging when Aster caught my wrist. She must have noticed what I was about to do and signaled me to stop. I realized that in my anger I would only end up ruining the concert for Aster and creating a scene. So I went back, clutching Aster's hand and letting go of my anger.

After the next two songs, Albert had gone on to play one of his hits, making the crowd go absolutely wild. I refused to wait anymore. I held her hand and safely walked out through the exit.

"I am so sorry that you could not enjoy the concert," I said. "But there's no way you are putting yourself on the line for it."

"It's okay. I didn't expect so much of push and pull."

"But you really wanted to attend it, I know."

"It's totally cool, Charlie," she said. "Do I look unhappy to you?"

"Pretty much," I nodded.

I wished I could have done something about it; arranged tickets in the front row or get her passes for the VIP box.

I hated the disappointment on her face.

I tried making up for the fun she missed by taking her to her favourite sidewalk café. We had only settled ourselves when a couple sitting next to us noticed us and came over. It was when they introduced themselves that I understood that they used to be Aster's classmates and were shocked to see her after such a long time. William and Isabella were engaged and were going to get married in a few months. Their excitement was supremely tangible from their body language. Aster proudly introduced me as her man, and it took Isabella by surprise. She said that now when she finally had a boyfriend, she seemed to have finally put rest to her feminine tantrums. This was quite suggestive of the insecure girl in Aster who had refused to fall in love.

As Isabella went on to hype her surprise, I was learning more about Aster. All this time she had kept to herself, not talking much to anyone. She would warmly welcome people, but never mix up with them. A number of guys in her class had approached her but she declined to hang out with any of them. Consequently, everyone had given her the tag of the 'Ice Queen'.

I was amused. A human being is much deeper than we can identify with our sight. If one is not in capacity to behold them from every aspect, which no one on earth surely is, one should not judge them with one's one dimensional view. Remarks and comments always hurt and bring woeful effects, and people need to understand that human nature is an ultimate upshot of circumstances. Every person is brought up in a different environment. Even if a homogeneous predicament is thrown to two people with similar resources to tackle them, the results will not be the same.

I wondered how Aster had dealt with such stuff. Everybody wants to be understood, and at times it is even more important than being loved. To have been raped at a tender age and then be catapulted in the hell of criticism for a perceived arrogance – life certainly had been tough and no less than hell for Aster.

Isabella's surprise at her being in a relationship gradually converted into enthusiasm to know about the man that she had finally accepted. I introduced myself as a simpleton from the beautiful village of Lugaar and who on realizing that it wasn't feasible to stay back as opportunities were extremely limited had been encouraged to move to Etiole.

Then came the much dreaded question about my family. I lied that my parents were running a small business back in the village. Aster shot a surprising look at me, but didn't question me at that moment.

I also told her that I was working as a salesman. Isabella and William had seemed to be disappointed hearing that.

"Charlie is a brilliant writer. Though he never talks about it," Aster added.

"No, it's nothing like that. I am just another man who can write, that's it."

"He is just being modest," she said clutching on to me.

Suddenly feeling uncomfortable with the course of conversation, I tried to divert the topic from me to complementing William and Isabella. Both were really happy to talk about themselves as it was quite evident that they were really happy with the present status of their relationship.

Isabella was unstoppable – telling us about the day they had met each other and how subtly and sweetly they had fallen in love with each other eventually and how excited they were as they were to be doctors soon. It was pleasant to hear about two people in the same profession getting married to each other. Such couples tend to understand each other's work and priority, and eventually to understand one another better.

She went on to talk about the brilliant plans for their wedding day. They had reserved a big palace in the countryside where their friends and families would start pouring in two days prior to the big fat wedding. Isabella also flaunted the beautiful diamond ring that William had presented to her when he had popped the question. It was a five thousand pound ring, much more than the entire savings of my life. While Aster was extremely happy for her friend, I wasn't.

I was constantly asking myself whether I would ever be able to do the same for her. Would she be so excited for her wedding?

To me, she wasn't some random girl who I was dating, to have sex with and move on. I wanted to be with her forever and more. I wanted to love her limitlessly. I wanted to commit the span of my life to make her feel happy.

Right now I was her boyfriend, but I wanted to be better than that for her. I wanted to be her hero.

It took ages for Isabella and William to finally realize that we both were patiently waiting for them to stop narrating any more of their wedding details. Perhaps out of courtesy, William extended an invitation to me for their wedding, though I seriously doubted whether there was any point because the kind of description spree Isabella was on, I was already aware of the colour of the curtains, carpets, grass and even the glasses that would be used to serve water and of the uniform of the chauffeurs driving the wedding guests. I was pushed into saying yes because Aster seemed very eager and I couldn't say no to her. Finally, when there was nothing left to talk about, the glorious couple left in a luxurious two-seater sports car while I had to drop my girl in a cab. That did wonders to my already deflated ego and confidence.

Even if Aster had noticed the sudden change in my mood, she chose to be kind about it and let me wallow in my own sorrow. She didn't force me to open up my feelings or share what I was thinking. She was kind enough to not even mention her friends or marriage though I wondered if she knew what was bothering me.

I dropped her and left without having the heart to meet her eyes. I was afraid that she would read my failures and debilities that had downrightly taken all over me suddenly. And I couldn't let that happen because I was too much of a coward to accept them in her face. I left her standing on the steps of her hostel, desperately wanting to talk to me.

I walked without bothering where the roads took me, letting my mind battle with the thoughts that were burning me deep inside. I was introspecting whether I deserved to be with Aster, someone whose life with me could be like a punishment.

Meeting Isabella and William made me feel that Aster belonged to a different section of society. With a better bunch of people and surely not a poor little orphan like me, struggling to fulfill the basic needs of life. Taking note of my own self, I did not even know what the coming day of my life would bring me. How I was going to tackle something really horrible standing in my way. Something like a serious accident or a fatal disease? I had nothing in my pocket and what if all of this happened to the ones I loved? Was I going to be able to get them out of it? No. Not at all. So my thoughts started to revolve around whether I should I leave Aster so that she could enjoy a better future with somebody else.

But then what good would a break up do Aster in her present condition? I reflected over it deeply, coming to a decision that I must at least try for her sake. Yes, that was what was to be done. That was the absolute right thing. So now what was I going to do to turn everything around? What really was the tool to be picked? I wasn't getting an answer though. Despite pressing my mind, I was clueless. I looked up in the sky. Maybe the moon or the stars that shone brightly could give me a solution. I was waging a war with myself to quickly figure a way to give Aster everything. Everything she would ever want to have.

That night when I reached home, I was terribly down, feeling shunned at the hands of the universe that was only being a bystander to my condition. I had nothing to offer Aster. It was Ed who opened the door for me. Something in my face must have given away the fact that I had had a terrible day as only seconds later he came back with two glasses of wine into the room.

"Here, this may help you," Ed said extending the glass to me.

Now call it being in a bad state of mind or some reflex action, I had downed the drink even before Ed could sit down.

"Wow! I thought one glass was going to work for you. Let me get the whole bottle."

Ed was right. I didn't open my mouth until we both were completely drunk and had finished through an entire bottle.

"Who am I? A big nothing," I said. "I have nothing to give Aster except poetic promises. No shelter, no good future... nothing special."

"This is your fight, Charlie. You accompanied me to Etiole to see me chase my dreams. But now, you have your destination waiting for you."

"What if I fail? I am so used to my efforts never fructifying."

"In the last seven years, how much effort have you made? Tell me honestly."

"I never got a chance to do anything. They ended my academic career, giving me a blank transfer certificate."

"Be practical, buddy. Even if they hadn't given it to you, we never had the money or any scholarship to attend college."

"Yeah, but..."

"Look, if you really love that girl, then at least do something for her sake. Do you want to sell products that will fetch you nothing in the end? And do you want your girl to live with you under a bridge in the fucking cold?"

"No Ed. Not even in my worst nightmare can I offer her that. I only want the best for her."

"Your mere saying or wanting won't do, Charlie. You must do something about it, something truly special."

For the next couple of days, I spent the major part of my time assessing the easiest schemes of becoming rich. I did substantial groundwork about the businesses and prospects that defined most rags to riches stories. But my findings were extremely depressing. To me, anything that had the potential of giving me massive wealth seemed to be far beyond my knowledge and competency. I also felt it was getting lucky rather and nothing else.

With not a single task that I could handpick to do, I was frustrated. But then, how could I give up? Whatever I wanted to accomplish was all for Aster. For a girl whom I loved from the core of my heart. For a girl whose smile always gave me a reason to fight and a reason to try harder each day. Whenever I looked into her eyes, I saw hope. A hope of being truly cared for by me.

Though she had all of me in every way she wished to have, yet I was questioning myself: Is it merely enough to support a comfortable life? Imagining her being deprived of anything used to push me in the dumps. I was longing to go back to Lugaar with her, wanting to spend the rest of our lives together around hills of my village. But I didn't want to return to that ignored part where I used to live – that room with the broken roof and those streets with the infinite puddles. I wanted to buy a home for her. A home where she could live peacefully. We could begin a family and finally find sanctity in it. But how would I make it all possible? That was the question troubling me continuously.

Amidst all this chaos, I had to be present in the office to report my progress for the ongoing month. The area sales manager shot a look at me as I entered his cubicle, immediately asking me to surrender everything that belonged to the company. I was stunned by his words.

"But sir, what happened? My performance in sales and grievance handling has always been good. In fact, you were the one who told me so a week ago."

I was barely holding it together with the last ounce of hope slipping out of my hands.

He looked at me sternly and said, "I do not know how many people you have been making your sales from, but the majority are complaining that they have never seen your face. We can't afford to have any of these complications in our organization. Therefore, submit our property and leave."

Despite my repeated requests, he was not moved. He stayed firm to his decision and I was thrown out of the organization. Distress, I tramped to Aster, giving her a call from the nearest public phone. She came running as she sensed something wrong from my shaky voice over the phone. I informed her that my job was gone and she needn't wait for me in the hospital anymore. I would look for a new job in a few days.

"But Charlie, you were born to be an author," she said. 'You aren't made for all this you are doing. That day what you wrote for me, I found it extraordinary. Enough for a girl to trust a man. If your words can move me, I believe, they can perhaps touch everyone. Please...please do consider writing again seriously."

"But I am only able to write on small useless topics that can't earn me a penny, Aster."

"Don't call them useless. Nothing is useless. Write what your heart yearns for, even if it's a few words."

"You don't understand. It's impossible to write after so many years."

"Impossibility is just a blasphemy that survives in exhausted human minds, Charlie. It is simply a hostile disorder planted by excuses. It puts limitation to excellence of the imagination. It truncates the power of love. Life means to see beyond the boundaries of possibility. That knack is what differentiates miracles from mere happenings."

Her words first made me realize how weak I was, and next ignited a spark of toughness in me. I looked at her wondering if this was how I must fight for the love, the trust and the immense confidence that Aster had in me.

Refusing to feel pliable by collywobbles of the coming day, I decided to make my present better. I reached my flat, unlocked the door and sat down to write. I scribbled down anything and everything that knocked against the door of my creativity: love, ambition, encounters, devotion, faith, and friendship.

I was so absorbed in writing that I hadn't realized that the sun had gone down until Ed jolted me awake from my writing reverie.

"Hey brother. How was your day?" he asked as he sat down on the chair.

"I got fired!" I replied with no regrets.

"Come again?"

"I have been fired, buddy."

"Are you kidding me?"

"No, I am serious."

"Holy shit! How did that happen?"

"Forget it."

"What do you mean by forget it?"

"It's over. Let's move on. Talking about it won't help."

It took time for that to sink in. "But what are you going to do now?"

"I am going to become a writer; won't be looking for a job now," I declared

"Excuse me? Both of us will not be able to live here in Etiole, Charlie. Neither I am making any money, nor you."

"I will leave. I don't need this city to be a writer. I only need a peaceful room," I said.

"Can you please look into my eyes and repeat what you just said?"

"I said I will leave. I don't need this city to be a writer. I just need a room that is peaceful."

"Wonderful. That was what after all these years I deserve to be hearing from you, right?"

That evening went down in a heated exchange between both of us. It wasn't my decision to quit looking for a job that boiled him so much but the fact that I said that I would leave Etiole. It didn't come from my heart though. I just happened to say it without thinking, but it hurt Ed a lot.

"Fine then. What are you waiting for? Just pick your bag and go wherever you want to."

He stormed out of the room and I was left sitting there, guilty of having hurt him unintentionally.

Few hours later when Ed's fury calmed down, I went to him with a beer in my hand as a peace offering. He didn't say anything, but was very upset and wouldn't talk to me.

"Ed, I am sorry for what I said."

"Go wherever the hell you want to. But don't talk to me anymore."

"I am really sorry, brother," I said. "And since when have you started taking my words to heart. You know that was just a slip of tongue."

"Considering leaving me is a slip of tongue, huh? Do you remember when we came here, we had one firm decision? That irrespective of what comes or goes, we shall always stand by each other. In our years together, we fought, cared, loved, and blamed each other, but never on a single day I can recall, that either of us uttered anything about leaving."

"I just messed up, brother. I didn't mean it. You always said that I don't have a vision, and I was going to end up being just another person meant to spend his destined years. But now, I seriously have a goal in my life. I want to become a writer and I brutally want to make this comeback count."

"Charlie, we only have resources to last for a year or two, but what after that?"

"So should I focus on a job, you mean?"

"No, idiot. What I mean is that you should go travel that extra mile and do both – a job and writing. Because you know very well that with acting auditions, I practically can't do two things at the same time. So what you essentially need to understand is that my responsibility is somewhere placed on you."

"Don't worry about that, Ed. I will take the challenge. Trust me, our lives are in for a change, and they will be different within a year from now. And you know what, love is an inexplicable remedy. People who fall in love, never fail," I said downing my drink.

"I hope so too, Charlie. But I feel if you are going for something in life, you must do it without brooding over the chances of your failing at it. Do prepare yourself for wanting to give up on many occasions. But no matter what, you must keep going, or both of us will end up miserably."

"Keep showing me the way, and we certainly will make big in life," I said while toasting our drinks.

Though I did assure Ed that our times were in for a good change, I was personally not convinced. However, I didn't want my pessimism to shadow his ambitions. But yes, on the other hand, I also knew that even my focus had to be unwavering and there was not a day to be wasted grumbling. My major obstacle until now had been no proper idea to dwell upon. I was only scribbling whatever my heart wanted to pen down, and that perhaps lasted merely a hundred or two hundred words at each new attempt. I wondered how they were going to be of any use to me and then remembering what Ed said, I had begun to feel the heat of the present moment's demand and I definitely had started to push myself harder than ever before.

"Why don't you buy yourself a laptop?" Jonathan said, picking the discarded sheets of my writing spread all over the floor.

"Is it going to be of help?" I asked peeping out of my diary.

"These days most writers use them," he said. "It's more convenient. You have the vocabulary fix in it which makes writing easier and faster. Plus, you don't have to overwrite or rewrite words like you have to do on sheets."

I thought for a moment. I was apprehensive as I had never used one ever, but decided to give it a try. The next day, I went to a gadget shop in the hope of buying a small laptop which could run the typing software at a genuine speed. The price was however higher than what I could afford, therefore, I had to use Eugene's credit card to pay for it. I was finally in possession of a laptop.

The guys had all left for their jobs, including Ed who had an audition, so it was just me in the house. Taking advantage of being alone and the accompanying silence, I started typing out my thoughts and vision in the laptop. Eventually one page led to another and before I knew the sun had set for the day and I had finished three chapters in a go.

I never noticed the guys returning or the little party they were enjoying until they had to literally pick me up from my seat and force me to have dinner. That was when I realized that I hadn't had a morsel of food the entire day; I was so engrossed in writing.

It turned out to be a daily routine for me to shut myself up completely, absorbed in writing. The guys had to check on me in between to make sure that I had not passed out of exhaustion or evaporated in my seat and it was at times like that when I truly cherished the warmth of family that these guys provided me with.

"I feel you should add more lines to this paragraph," Aster suggested, casting a brief look into my laptop.

It was Sunday and we were in a bus, travelling to Bratten, a coastal area that was a hundred miles away from Etiole. At some point, the guys must have been concerned over my state. They had called Aster and she dragged me out of home to take a walk and get some fresh air, which then turned out to be this Sunday trip to Bratten. Although she was not a fan of the idea at first, she eventually let me carry my laptop with me. She was enjoying the view while I was busy writing about whatever came to my mind.

The bus dropped us a few minutes away from the beach so we walked the rest.

The scenery was breathtaking, and the rejuvenating sound of the waves crashing onto the rocks made us feel like we were friends with the ocean. The sand was fine – cold and velvety under our naked feet. As the clouds moved, the glittering rays of the sun fell on the never ending sheet of water, turning the seascape into something even more delectable.

"My God! The beach is punctuated with some smoking hot girls, huh!" I said.

Aster looked at me making a freakish, jealous face. But before she could say anything, I added putting my arms around her shoulder, "Nonetheless, the most beautiful one is beside me and she's all I'll ever need."

She hugged me and innocently pointing towards a sand hut, said, "This will be our home one day."

"That day will be the best day of my life, Aster," I said locking her in my arms and planting a gentle kiss on her forehead.

I wished every single day could be the same as that morning. No worries of the future, no regrets from the past, far from the intrusion of the noisy world and in the arms of the one you love.

Together we walked in the limitless mirror of the sky, holding our hands and looking at each other. We smiled and felt safe in each other's presence.

Love is such a pure thing to be felt and to be lived. While life guarantees death, love promises a blissful voyage through it. Aster had filled my life with all colours of joyousness. I knew that even if I lost every battle, she would stand by me. She was an angel to me, who had transformed my life in ways I could have never imagined.

It was only three years back when I was fighting depression and developing suicidal tendencies. But now here I was, sitting on a rock with the love of my life, watching the birds fly to the place where sun and water meet.

"Let's get you a cab to take you home safey," I said after we reached Etiole.

"Can we please walk? I want to be with you for some more time," Aster said, pulling my hand and dragging me on the pathway along with her.

"Why do I have to be on my toes to reach your face?"

"So that, you don't have to bend to rest your head on my chest."

"I wish I was as tall as you Mr Six Feet," she said with a smile.

"That would give us giant kids."

"True," Aster said, laughing out loud.

"Aster, I want to marry you someday and have you by my side till I die."

"Sounds like a good plan."

"I love you, Aster," I said, looking into her eyes. "Each time I see you happy, I feel as if nothing can ever go wrong."

"I love you, Charlie. Thanks for being mine." She perched high on her toes to kiss me.

We stopped there on the road, kissing. Suddenly a car appeared and stopped dangerously close to us.

The back door opened and a girl was pushed out. Her body fell on the road like a ragged doll. She was naked. The car rushed away. The body of the girl had been scratched with a sharp instrument and she had serious wounds all over her. I was unable to decipher what was happening. Aster jumped to check whether she was still breathing. We quickly covered her body with our jackets and looked around for help. Nobody stopped. No car. No truck. No bus. We couldn't wait for any more time as the girl seemed to be running out of breath.

I picked her up and ran to the hospital as fast as I could.

"Get a stretcher! Get a stretcher!" Aster shouted repeatedly as we hurriedly climbed the ramp of the emergency block.

My shirt was soaked in blood now and I couldn't dare look at it as I would have frozen at the sight. Running harder and harder, I could feel the girl's breathing getting horribly low. A stretcher was brought by the staff and I gently placed her on it with a little help from them. Aster went along to take care of the girl while I stood outside, waiting.

It was almost dawn when she came out. She held my finger and kept walking until we reached a place where there was nobody around. She had tears in her eyes.

"Is the girl alright?" I asked

She shook her head.

"What happened?"

She was quiet and seemed to have gone numb.

"What happened?"

"She was raped," she finally answered while breaking into tears, stopping. "And the scratches you saw on her skin have been made by a screw driver."

I tried to console her, but failed. I knew that this particular incident was reminiscent of what she had been through, and perhaps that's why she was so disturbed.

"What wrong have we girls done? Are we so heinous that we have to be brutally dealt with? Don't we have a heart? Don't we feel the pain? Only because we are delicate, does it give licence to boys to overpower girls and fulfill their animal like desires. That girl, she is dead. We weren't able to look into her parents' eyes and tell them what had happened to her. If we give them a detailed account of what their daughter had gone through, they would die of shock."

She began sobbing and couldn't speak anymore.

It was a terrible situation. There was nothing that I could have said to calm her down, and then what could one say in such matters? As bad as it sounded, the fact was that it was what was happening around us daily and nothing was done about it. The reason why these activities were on the rise was because people were focusing on becoming good engineers, clever business tycoons, efficient doctors, acclaimed writers, genius mathematicians, but no one was bothered about becoming a good human being. And since the element of morality has taken a back seat in our everyday system, things weren't meant to get any better.

Then on the other hand we had nations swamped with weapons, building an army, being diplomatic, working to be superpowers, but who wants to consolidate on making civilized citizens? None.

The following morning when I sat down to write, I began recollecting the incident. Aster's cries were unstoppably echoing in my ears. Realizing Aster's past and thinking of that girl's death, I began typing. When my fingers stopped, I looked at what I had written.

A girl is not a trophy to be won. The beauty she possesses isn't a product to be consumed. The sacrifices she makes aren't brainless. The kindness she exhibits is no subject of pranks. She is delicate. She is sensitive. She takes all the violence and abuses. Not because she is intimidated by anyone's outburst. But she is patiently waiting for her love to get noticed. She is an ocean of benevolence. She will care for us even when we don't reciprocate. Let's treat her well. She never asks for it. She deserves it.

I kept gazing at the screen. I could hear my breath and my heart beating faster. I finally had the answer to what my novel would be about. It was going to about Aster – her life and the agitation she wasn't able to let go. Yes, it was the finest answer to what Aster had asked me once, 'What had managed to touch the veritable extremity of my heart?'

At that moment I felt that this subject and this particular novel had to be much more than my materialistic dreams. And most importantly, for me, it ought to have the competence to evoke that much needed question of change. Because being an artist or a writer isn't only about finding fun in our imaginative work built in an unreal world. It was more about taking that gift thankfully while working towards changing the world into a better place.

On the first page, I entered the title *The Crumbled Gender.* Because instead of treating this class of sex well, they are, I guess, considered a lesser human being who are raped, tortured, manhandled, abused, burnt and subjected to everything that in every sense is barbaric.

Words began to flow and I was typing lightning quick. It wasn't like I had to raise my head up, think for several hours in a row and a write few words and wait for the next idea to complement it. I had seen and felt it all. The way Aster's childhood was destroyed, the manner in which the girl was treated had shaken me immensely. I had so much to tell, so much to share and a hell lot to change. My message was going to be simple and loud: Respect girls, they are meant to be treated well. The one who does deserves to be called a man.

The story had become my obsession those days. I couldn't let any minute go waste without thinking about fresh ideas to be penned down. Quite frankly, I had turned into an absent minded man who was very difficult to talk to. It happened during the nights as well. My mind was lost in deep thoughts, completely cut off from what was happening around me.

I wasn't bathing, I wasn't eating, and I wasn't going out much, but still I was getting an absolute thrill. One like never before. Gradually, I began to encounter peculiar learning experiences while working my script out. There were days where I sat down from early morning till afternoon without successfully committing to paper a single thought. And then there were days I could finish around a thousand odd words with no extra effort. But amidst all this, these new experiences I was going through, I felt as if I was a wanted man or perhaps I had gone back to being the person that all of us are naturally entitled to become – full of thoughts of changing the world, of contributing in my own special way to make the earth a better place to live in.

Nonetheless, most importantly, I never, not even for a single minute ever forgot to acknowledge the love of Aster being the reason behind awaiting the good things. She was that someone to hold my hand, someone waking up beside me and smiling seeing me peacefully asleep, thinking she was fortunate to have me because I deeply loved her. I had never imagined all this would ever come my way.

A month passed since I had passionately started off with the book, and I had written thirty-two thousand words by this time. I was confident of finishing the story by the end of the next month. I was halfway through and since publishing happened to be an industry that moved at a snail's pace, I thought that by the time I get any positive response, I should have finished with the complete manuscript and that would have saved me a lot of time. So I felt it was time to put my book through the initial process of publishing.

Since Jonathan was working in a publishing company, I requested him to acquaint me with the process of getting my book in print. He told me about an agent named Robert Smith – one of the big shots of the industry known for his ruthlessness, and more importantly, for being notoriously famous for disgracefully rejecting most of the manuscripts he used to receive. I sent him my work – a brief synopsis and three sample chapters through post, waiting to either get rejected or being completely ignored. However, eight days later, a strange thing happened. I was busy with the book when Johnny came to tell me that Robert Smith wanted me to meet him in his office.

"Why has he called me? Does that mean he has accepted my work?" I asked with a tiny ray of hope.

"Don't be so happy. Or happy at all. He often calls proposal senders to nail them. Takes a lot of pleasure messing with writers he thinks aren't fit to write and still dare to."

That was baffling. That sort of behaviour. How could a sane man do such a thing? I mean, he could ignore the rejected stuff and carry on. But why the need to humiliate someone? Especially someone like me who was already so nervous.

I felt a sinking feeling in my stomach, something that I couldn't explain. My fear was beyond the thinkable and I had my fingers tightly crossed. I was all prepared for the bashing of a lifetime but at the same time, I was hoping against hope to have gotten through. Because the prize was so big. Not merely was it getting published but it was a new life to me. A new birth. Like a new age.

The next day I ended up in Robert smith's office, completely shaking with nervousness and anticipation of what was to happen. I barely paid attention to the giant office as all my thoughts were revolving around what I would do if he trashed the work that I had put so much effort into.

Robert Smith was quite professional and didn't care about introductions or making me feel comfortable. Asking me to sit down, he jumped directly to business.

"We went through your script, and quite frankly it's a decent enough story. Hand us your complete manuscript and we will represent you along with charging a commission of twenty percent on whatever sales you make."

"When do you want the whole manuscript?"

"If you have brought it along with you, you can hand it to me right now and we are good to go."

My manuscript was only half done and I was definitely going to need more days to complete it. I wasn't going to lie about my work or make an excuse to be back later. So I told him the truth.

"Sir, I am only halfway through the book."

"How many more days will you need?" he asked with not much change in his emotions.

"One month, at max," I said.

"Are you sure about it?"

"Never been surer."

"Alright then," he said. 'We will give you a month to come up with the finished manuscript."

"I am really thankful, Mr Smith," I said as I got up and shook hands with him.

It was stupendous to hear that my novel had been undertaken to be represented before even being finished. I could not have asked for more. It was so great to think that in a matter of a few months, I was going to have my dream realized.

♦

A few days later, Edwin came running up to my room and since it was a weekday, none of the boys were in the house.

"What happened? Why are you so incredibly happy?"

"Guess what happened?" he asked excitedly.

I thought for a while. "You stole match tickets?"

"No, idiot. Guess again," he said.

"You found a hundred pound note lying somewhere?"

Ed was beginning to get annoyed. "No. Guess again."

"You got your legs waxed?"

"Did I come to Etiole to have hair free legs, you prick?"

"You got a role in a movie?"

"So finally you get it, huh?"

"Are you…are you kidding me?"

"We did it, Charlie," he said, pulling his advance check out of his pocket and waving it in the air.

"We did it!" I shouted as I ran to hug him.

Two boys who had come in shoddy clothes and a few pounds to Etiole were advancing.

What a journey this was turning out to be! Simply marvelous! Our lives were truly changing.

"Looks like we will have to go to Eden Apartments to book a flat for ourselves," I said, remembering our first night in Etiole.

"It will happen soon, very very soon, brother," Ed answered.

"Tell me about your role, man. I am dying to know about it."

"The first thing you should know is that around thousand people auditioned for this role, and it's your brother who is finally going to be playing it."

"That's incredible." He had lived up to my expectations. "Tell me more." I was dying to know.

"Basically, I am playing an assistant to a con-man who is going to con the con man."

"So that makes you the best con-man in the movie?"

"Yeah!"

We hugged each other and jumped all over the place in joy.

"Seems so unbelievable, right?" I stated, settling down on the mattress. "I was going to live under your shadow. But here I am, writing once again."

"I cannot be happier for you, Charlie," he said. "By the way, how much more of the book is left to be done?"

"Just the last chapter."

"Congratulations, brother! You have pulled it off so gracefully."

"Thank you, buddy. You have to be surely given a lot of credit for this. You are the reason why I am in Etiole in the first place."

"You are getting what you deserve, buddy. I am just glad to be a part of it."

"You know Charlie, I was kind of missing Claire today," Ed added. "It's been months since I saw her last."

"Why don't you take some time out, and go meet her?"

"It's not really possible."

"Did you tell her about your movie role?"

"Yeah, she was really happy. I could literally hear her jumping when I informed her. She has almost packed her bags for the premiere, she says."

"The girl's quite curious, huh?"

"I want to buy a home and bring her here."

"And I want to go back to Lugaar," I said. "It's peaceful there.'

"Peaceful"? He laughed. "Almost every day we have terrorists storming in from the other side of the border killing the innocents, and you find it peaceful."

"But it's our home, isn't it?'

He stood wondering for a while, looking here and there searching for an answer.

"Now there is no logic good enough to rip apart this particular emotion, you know." He finally gave up. "Anyway, have you seriously thought about it?"

"Yes, I have. But I'll keep coming here for holidays though," I said. "Four of us will have incredible celebrations each time we get together."

"You know, Charlie, the most painless task in this world would be to form large groups of people sharing common reasons for being unhappy, but the toughest would be to discover a teeny-weeny group, sharing a unanimous reason for a good laugh."

"So?" I asked.

"Welcome to the group of the happy ones, brother," he answered, winking.

We hugged each other again as both of us were insanely overjoyed with what life was offering us.

It was a cloudy morning and the gentle gush of air was filliping me to start. I picked my laptop and went to the nearest park to wrap up my work. I sat under a tree, took some deep breaths and began to type. I had completely lost track of time and my creation was almost at the brink of its completion. My life was never going to be the same humdrum of sadness for me. I was going to be an author – successful or failed, I didn't know, but unquestionably the one who sooner or later was going to matter.

As rays of the sun sharpened, the heat took over the entire place, though making no difference to my rock solid focus that had already reached its vertex. I was savoring each moment that I took in weaving new ideas out of sheer fantasy. It was an amazing feeling because I knew, I truly knew that I was going to love reliving these moments, time and again, recalling every step to my transformed life.

The gentle morning was replaced by a merciless noon. It blinded you so harshly that on throwing a look to the farthest point, you saw nothing but blinding white rays. I was drenched in my own sweat, but despite that, I was determined to finish my writing as I was that close to wrapping up my book. All this while, whenever I had felt tired and the thoughts of stopping came into my mind, I would pump myself up with thoughts of Aster – her smile, and her ability to make others smile worked far better than any dreams of receiving fame or money for my book.

Seven hours of sitting and writing had brought an end to my book and *The Crumbled Gender,* my first book was ready to be sent to the editor. I punched the air in joy and got up recalling how a year ago, the thought of me ever writing a book was perhaps only wild imagination.

Walking back, I felt high spirited, absolutely ecstatic and excited. It was only a good marketing plan that had to kick in now. My rumbling stomach made me stop by a food junction on my way. I ordered a cheese sandwich and coffee for myself. Till the time they got my order ready, I decided to work on my author's note, acknowledgement and other companion pages of the book. Halfway through my writing, I was interrupted by a flashing laser on my right that indicated that my order was ready. I left my seat and went to collect my breakfast. I happily picked it up and took my seat. Apart from the newly brought food, my table was empty.

My laptop was missing!

I checked back and forth in panic. It was nowhere to be seen. I ran out checking whether someone had taken it, but I couldn't find anyone. Unable to decipher what had just happened, I ran in and out, completely paranoid as curious spectators stared at me.

Feeling utterly disappointed, hopeless and above all angry, I screamed at the staff.

"I had kept my laptop here. Where the hell is it?"

"What are you saying, sir?" A member of the staff asked, trying to calm me down.

"I had kept my laptop here," I yelled pointing towards my table. "Where on earth is it now?"

The entire staff gathered around me. They probed about the brand and colour of my laptop and dispersed after listening to the specifications. Wistfully, nobody came back successful.

"What kind of a place is this? Get me my laptop or I'll kill all of you, every single one of you," I wailed.

"Sir, please don't shout. We are looking for it," the manager said in a very low voice.

"Call the god damn cops!" I yelled at them.

I kept checking the place in anxiety until the cops reached. The people inside the cafe had all been stopped from moving out. I expected the thief to be traced now, but when the cops came out and told me that cameras weren't working and people inside didn't have it, I went crazy. My anguish had turned my entire face red.

"Sir, we will get you a new laptop. Today itself," the manager said. "Perhaps an advanced version to what you were using."

"Are you a fucking idiot or what?" The pitch of my voice was at its peak. "If I don't find mine, I'll kill you without having any mercy on you. So go to hell, I don't care, but get me mine. Right now!"

The cops had had enough of listening to my rants.

"Listen, dude. Your gadget has been stolen, we understand that, but your ranting can land you in all sorts of trouble. Better leave this place and stay in touch with us. That's it."

I was unable to believe what had just happened to me. I kept telling myself again and again that this was just a bad dream and that I shouldn't worry. And it was going to end very soon. But nothing of that sort happened. I roamed the streets till dark, getting shattered moment after moment, unable to let the robbery sink in.

My time in the world had never been an easy walk, I thought. I had struggled each day to earn. I used to work fourteen to fifteen hours in a bakery and had no interaction with the world beyond it. When I stepped out of it, I fell in love. Surprisingly, I was loved back extensively. For the sake of that very love I had attempted to do something big and that was going in the right direction. And just when I thought I was reaching the finishing line, things fell apart once again for me.

Demolished and defeated, I landed outside a church. People were coming out in satisfaction, as if the one inside had assured them that all their problems would be solved. My heart pushed my feet to walk inside. I knelt down and tapped my hands on the floor,

"I give up…I give up…I give up!" I cried.

Tears were flowing out from my eyes like a river and I was completely devasted.

I folded my hands, requesting, begging, urging, warning and negotiating with God to find me my laptop. I swore to him that never in my life I would appear again with any request. My conscience said nothing was going to happen, but I wasn't prepared to admit it. No way!

I don't remember what exactly happened after that because when I opened my eyes, I was on my bed and Aster was sitting beside me and holding my hand.

"How did I reach here?" I asked.

She ran her hands through my hair and said, "You were lying unconscious in the church yesterday. How are you feeling now?"

"My laptop was stolen. It had all my hard work," I said, starting to shed tears.

"What is more important: your life or your writing?" she retorted. "What are you doing to yourself, Charlie? Can't you take care of yourself for me?"

"I am going to die if I don't find it."

"Don't say rubbish, Charlie!"

"You don't understand, Aster, I have nothing left to live for."

"Not even me?" she asked I had no answer to that.

"Charlie, promise me that you will not do anything stupid. Not even think of it."

I was too broken inside to listen to her words or even acknowledge them with a response.

"Charlie, promise me, please. Your silence is killing me."

I said nothing.

"Charlie, promise me."

I couldn't bring myself to say anything.

"Charlie, please. I beg of you. Promise me!"

"Yeah, alright," I said half-heartedly, without looking into her eyes.

"Not this way. Give me your hand and then promise."

I did what she asked. But internally, I was too numb to know what I was doing.

"Promise me that you won't do anything reckless and stupid."

"I already did, girl!" I shouted madly at her. "Do I have to promise you a million times? Can't you trust me in the first place?"

She got horrified at the way I had spoken to her. But she replied softly, "Love is giving away anything as many times it is asked for. So if it is in form of sacrificing or promising someone a million times, you must then promise me a million times."

I said nothing for a moment, realizing my mistake, and just kept looking into her eyes that reflected my pain.

"I am sorry, Aster," I said, tears welling up in my eyes again.

"It's okay. Charlie. I am always by your side. Always," she said, hugging me with all her love.

In the days that followed, I was in baffling agony, making countless trips to the cops and checking the status of my stolen gadget. I wasn't still able to digest my loss. It seemed as if I was only meant to go through ruthless struggles, that I was never destined to win. It took so much of me to write the book, but now it was all gone, evaporated as if it were mere droplets of water.

Running out of hope, I became vulnerable, getting irritated by minor things that otherwise I would have easily ignored. My eyes had swollen up due to my sleepless nights and I looked like a drug addict. I was still hoping against hope that a miracle could occur and fix everything. Maybe by my laptop would be discovered and I could breathe happily again. A month later when I, on Aster's insistence agreed to visit a psychiatrist, I discovered that I was in depression and needed help. He prescribed medicines that used to put me to sleep for hours.

I could not decipher the purpose of taking them because they weren't clearly making me happy; it was Aster who was rather doing it. She didn't have the best of sense of humor, but see what love does to people. She would do everything and anything to bring a smile on my face. From slipping while climbing on the bed to making funny sounds or intentionally dropping ice cream on her dress and making cute faces, she did them all – everything that she could possibly think of. Despite her efforts not fructifying, she never gave up and never got mad at me for not letting it go. She was that good to me, that understanding.

Failing to get over it, I developed a habit of switching off the lights and sitting in the dark for hours. Aster would come and take me out with her, asking me to never do it, but I would seldom listen to her as it reminded me of my status in the world – undesirable. Completely undesirable.

In between all this, Edwin had to leave for a shoot. He had decided to skip it so that he could be with me, but since I knew how important it was for his career, I forced him to leave rather than let my bad luck grab a hold on him as well. He had a life beyond me, and it was time for him to focus on it.

Two days later, Aster came to our house reminding me that Isabella's wedding was in three days. I almost said 'no' to accompanying her to the wedding as I was sure that I wouldn't able to face the crowd. But eventually I said yes as I didn't want to be a disappointment for my girl and it was the least I could do after all the trouble I had given her.

We together made it to the venue a day prior to the wedding. It was taking place in a jaw dropping castle that tyrannized the entire landscape. Standing like an unconquered emperor fenced by its herculean army of mountains, the five-stories were entrenched with a beautiful pond right in front with a timber bridge going above it. It took one to the grand wooden door on the ingress that opened up to a spectacular view of a tiered fountain and captivating varieties of trees like judas and sycamore. Inside the house, the ceilings held chandeliers that were stylishly patterned using sleek logs. The marble on the floor throughout the place narrated various stories of art and bravery through the incredible pictures carved on them. It was truly a blue-blooded wedding affair that was going to add glory to the memories of two lives.

William and Isabella's families warmly received us as we entered and helped us locate our room which was nothing less than a mini house in itself. It had a hall, a beautiful king sized bed and boxy cushy looking sofas that would entice you to comfortably fall on them and lose yourself in the awe of the glorious paintings that hung on the four walls.

Then in the evening, when we went downstairs for a party organized by William and Isabella, Aster went around introducing me to many of her classmates. All of them appeared to be commendably rich and nifty, and had this enhanced sense of superiority. I was feeling nervous and uncomfortable being around them, but I didn't let that show on my face.

The behaviour of not just Aster's friends, but almost everyone towards me was quite cold. After a courtesy hello, nobody seemed to notice my presence. Not knowing me and hence not talking was one thing, but an awkward silence whenever I passed by any group was a different one. I, therefore, limited myself to the room for the rest of the evening and during dinner, I retired to a corner in the dinner hall. One of Aster's classmates named Monty Pebbles walked up to me. I was sure that he was up to something as he had this crooked smile on his face.

"Hello, Mr Boyfriend," he said, singing and dusting the mud off from my shoulder.

I chose to ignore the taunt and poison in his words.

"You know ever since I have met you, I am unable to believe Aster's choice. What did she exactly find in you, or did you coerce her into a relationship with you, huh?"

I ignored him again, stealing my eyes from him this time.

"Your disheveled hair and untidy clothes and this smell! I wonder whom you take after – your mother or father. What do you think? Or are you just a fucking mixture of both the idiots who decided to give birth to you?"

His words rattled me. I felt like kicking him in the face and endlessly slapping him, but I did not want to create a scene before such an anticipated event. All I could do was to press my jaws in anger, stare at him for a moment and walk away.

He caught me by arm and propelled a chair in front of me.

"Look at the clothes you are wearing," he said grabbing my face. "Can't be even compared to a waiter's outfit."

I controlled myself again.

"Even if you sell yourself, you won't be able to buy the kind of clothes I wear. Notice the suit on me. It costs way more than your entire family's net worth. I have all the potential in the world to offer Aster."

Suddenly my anger transformed into embarrassment. It kind of pushed me to realize how I wasn't wanted at this place. He was taking me down in the mud, and disgracing me as much as he could.

"You brought her here in a god damn taxi. I came here drinking the finest wine in my limo. Few years later, you will not even have the money to afford a bicycle for your kids. But yes, I must admit that you seem quite an intelligent man, so before Aster kicks you out of her life because of your inabilities, why don't you consider leaving her and letting her have a better life with me?"

Monty Pebbles had been vying for Aster's attention for years, and she had rejected him each time. I knew it was in sheer jealousy that he was saying all those words to me, but I was vulnerable and gullible at that point and I wasn't in the right frame of mind to look at it from that angle. With everything already having gone so wrong, I took his words very seriously.

"Hope you are having a good time, both of you!" Aster said joining us. Her hair, falling to the left side of her pink gown made her look divine. For a moment I stood frozen, mesmerized by her beauty and radiance.

"We are having a hell of a time. Aren't we, Charlie?" Pebbles replied, winking at me. "By the way, what do you do, Mr Charlie?"

"He is a writer." Aster quickly replied for me.

"Wow! So how many books have you authored so far?"

"The thing is...." I began to say.

"His first book is coming out next year, Monty." Aster cut me short. "Charlie has authored a book on a beautiful subject. I am looking forward to seeing you guys reading it and telling me how my man writes."

"Your man? Oh come on, Aster," he said, guffawing. 'Nothing is official until its official."

"What are you talking about?"

"What I am talking about is the fact that I don't see you two as a couple," he said.

"Can you please excuse us for a while, Monty," Aster said, faking a smile and pulling me away.

"Listen, Charlie. This man is the biggest jerk you will ever face. Stay away from him and if he says anything to you that you don't like, do whatever you want to, but don't you dare tolerate him."

Aster kissed me then, and said that she would meet me later in the night as she had to go for the bachelorette party organized in a separate hall for all the young ladies.

After Aster left, I was heading back to my room when Monty crossed my path again.

"Hey waiter, what the fuck are you doing there?" Pebbles had returned with one of his drunken friends. "Why don't you have a tray in your hands? Go grab one and bring a wine for us."

"Pebbles, you are drunk. I am not a waiter," I said.

"You aren't a waiter? Then you must be a village guy who has stormed in here for free food."

"I don't want to get into an argument, Monty."

"Argument?" Monty asked. "Do you think you are worthy enough to have an argument with people like us? You uncivilized worm. Get your ass out of this place right now!"

"And if I don't, what are you going to do about it, huh?" I looked into his eyes, challenging him to say one more word and I was ready to knock his teeth down.

"Did your father not teach you how to behave with royal people, you prick?"

The result of those words would have been his death, so I chose to turn around and walk out of the room, controlling my anger once again and refusing to reply. But he held me by my collar and threw his wine on my face.

"I am so sorry. It was by mistake, brother. Someone pushed me," he said as the people around pause to look.

I returned to my room without uttering even a single word. I was cursing myself for having said yes to come for the wedding. Never had I felt so bad about myself before. I was poor, I didn't have money, I didn't have parents, my clothes were old, but what was my fault? And if Monty had all of them, what special thing had he done except inheriting a fucking legacy? I blamed God for the injustice and picking up a vase, I threw it against the wall angrily.

I turned back, looked at myself in the mirror and I could see big tears rolling down my red eyes. There were no counter arguments to what Monty had said to humiliate me. The two people who had created me had discarded me like bad quality toilet paper, then why blame the world for doing the same. Why blame the people to whom I meant nothing. I wanted to scream like I had done all my childhood, but what was the use.

There was a knock on the door and I wiped my face as I moved to turn the lights on. Before I could open the door, an envelope came flying from beneath the door. It hit the edge of my shoe and I bent down to pick it up. At the back of it was written:

Spend your night looking at the thing inside and wisely think who this girl belongs to.

A boy who wears faded clothes to parties or the boy who preserves the angelic look of this fairy?

I opened the envelope. It contained a photograph of the moment when I was standing with Aster and Monty Pebbles in the dinner hall. Fearing the inevitable, I covered myself with my hand in the photograph and looked at both of them. Then I covered him with my hand and looked at both of us. Incurably, there was an immense disparity that I noticed. She looked wonderful with him, while I...I looked like a mere waiter standing next to her. A waiter without a tray, like Pebbles had truthfully said.

What should I do? Should I really let her go, letting her be with a better man or make her a part of all misfortunes I'd encounter each day of my life?

♦

Life is like an athletic event. The rules are well-defined – precise and lucid. However, when there is a crisis, common-sense wobbles, leaving the player in cold sweat. Subsequently when things were meant to be addressed with a calm mind, a sudden move ruins it all.

On the wedding morning, I was standing on the terrace with Aster and Isabella. We were looking at the decorations being done in the courtyard and there, in the center, stood Isabella's and William's family having an animated conversation. They were all laughing, hugging each other, patting each other on the back, and having a good time.

"Over the years, you have missed being part of a family, Aster, haven't you?" Isabella said. "You stayed alone in the hospital when all of us used to go home for holidays. And how can I forget about you wishing to make up for those days by meeting your man's family. I am sure, very sure in fact that when you get married to Charlie, his parents will welcome you with an open heart and you shall get all the love you have missed throughout the years."

Her longing for a family slivered me into crumbs. Isabella did not know the truth about me, and she revealed something that I shouldn't have known. I absolutely had nothing to give to Aster – no money, no family, nothing. So did she deserve to be with a man like that? Should she be deprived of something that she could get from some other person? – These questions began to knock my head violently. Consequently, I decided that my time in her life was over. After the wedding, I was going to say goodbye to her. Forever. Because just like that old lady in the train had said, 'love is sacrificing, without letting the world know about it.'

During the wedding, everybody was happy, whereas I was wondering how to tell Aster that I was going to leave her for good. It was as tough as chopping a chunk of flesh from my own body. I was about to break the heart of the girl who made me feel needed in this world. The more I saw her, the tougher it was getting.

"Aster, I can't be with you. I am sorry," I said as we entered her room after wedding.

"What?"

"It's over between us. We both need to move on."

"What the hell are you saying?"

"Goodbye, Aster," I said, picking my bag, stealing my gaze from her.

"Wait!" She ran to me from the other side of the bed. "Did I do anything wrong? Please tell me," she pleaded.

"No you didn't. It's just that we can't be together anymore."

"Listen. I understand that you are going through a tough phase. Take some time. I know it must be hard and probably I was wrong forcing you to attend this wedding, I…"

"Aster stop! Look into my eyes, it's over between us," I said pushing her away and releasing my hand from her hold.

"Did somebody say something to you, Charlie? See, no matter what anybody says, you know how much I care for you. How much I love you. This is not you Charlie. This is not you talking…"

"Aster, don't be an idiot. Don't think that I am walking away because somebody said something. Get these silly thoughts out of your girlish mind."

"Then why are you doing this?" She clutched onto my hands firmly as she sobbed. "You remember the letter you wrote for me. Was it all a lie?"

"I don't know which letter you are talking about."

My words must have hurt her very bad because almost instantly she let go of my hand. I turned my back on her, unable to face her.

"Charlie, do you feel disgraced to be with me? Is that why you are being cruel to me? Are you mortified to be with a girl who was raped?"

I knew why she brought the 'raped girl' part in our conversation. She wasn't trying to win sympathy, she was aiming to save her relationship. But I had to forcefully use this as a tool to make her hate me.

"If you know the truth, why do you ask?"

"What?" I could hear her crumpling to the floor.

"You are a disgrace to be with, Aster. I will be ashamed to introduce you to my friends after we get married."

"The same friends who had seen us fall in love with each other, Charlie?"

"Yeah the same ones. I am ashamed. Is that clear enough for you Aster?"

"I don't understand, Charlie. Why?" She got up from the floor and forced me to look into her eyes which I tried avoiding for the fear of completely losing myself.

"You have known about me all this time, then why today? Didn't you tell me that you didn't care about my past and all you care about was the future? Our future?"

"There is no future, Aster and no 'ours' anymore. It's over," I tried to shove her away but Aster held me by my wrist making me face her.

"So what was that we had until now? What was that when you held me close? Held my hands promising me that you would always be there? Looked at me like I meant something to you? What were those promises all about? Those million promises?"

"Those were fake, Aster. Wake up. It's over. The sooner you realize it, the better. Don't waste your life around me.

"It was the final straw and I was struggling to keep it together, so I pushed Aster away and grabbed my bag to walk out of the room. But before I could do that, Aster had taken the bag away from me and had thrown it back on the bed

"Don't say that. You promised me that you would never let me go," Aster pleaded taking my hands.

"Yes I did, but I can't anymore. I can't be with you." I grabbed my bag again and started to move out, but Aster held my hands with all her strength. It was breaking my heart watching her trying to keep me from leaving.

"Aster, don't make it hard for both of us. Let me go," I said tugging at my hand to release it from her strengthening grip.

"No Charlie, listen to me. Don't do this to me. I promise. Whatever it is, we will work on it. I will work on it."

She wasn't letting me go. I was trying to push her away, but she only kept tightening her hold.

"Leave me, Aster. There is nothing you can do. Your past is way too heavy for me to drag around. I am sorry."

This time with all desperation, I pushed her away to free myself from her grip. Either it was the push or it was the sheer intensity of my words that made her lessen her grip.

"Charlie…." she fell on her knees crying.

"Have a nice life, Aster."

I rushed out of the door before she could grab me again, but I was sure that my heart was still left in the room with Aster. I could feel hollowness where my heart used to be.

Before leaving the castle, I had one more thing to do. I took a paper out of the same diary that Aster had given me and wrote a letter addressed to Monty Pebbles.

Hey Rich Guy,

Not that you need to understand that Aster is the most beautiful girl in the world, which by the way she seemingly is, but what you really need to know is that she is the most wonderful human being who walks around, genuinely caring for everyone's happiness. And an even more amazing thing about her is that she is never diminished by all the difficulties she has had to pass through. Unlike all of us, she astonishingly maintains to be what she has chosen to be.

However, despite how mature and compassionate she may be, she needs to be loved unconditionally. There has to be someone to tell her that it may not be everyone, but there definitely is someone who understands her to the core. But like you said, she also needs to savour all comforts in life. She deserves to go to the most exotic locations, wear the best designer clothes, have a wonderful home, which I certainly can never give her. So I realize my mistake and leave Aster to you. Keep her happy in every single way possible.

If I was ever rude to you, I apologize for it. Don't ever be angry at her for being with a man like me. I just conned her into a relationship, and you know very well that girls are emotional beings, and we men are skilled artisans at manipulating them.

Keep her happy always and have a good life with her.

With no wish to see you both again,

Charlie

It feels like dying when you have to return to the point from where you had started with a billion hopes and dreams, and even worse to find no courage to re-start because time has prudently tailored you to believe that you won't ever reach the finish line. My friends were shell shocked with what had happened to my relationship. Initially, they had refused to believe me, thinking that I was pulling a prank on them. But when they found my wretched expressions unchanged, they were eventually convinced.

It hurt them badly, I could see.

After a mournful silence, each of them sternly instructed me to go back and apologize to Aster, but I refused to. I refused each time they rationally attempted to convince me about my mistake. They argued that I was on a self-destruction spree and that I was being a victim of my own groundless thoughts building out of the lack of courage. Honestly, I was offended by that argument, feeling as if they intentionally wanted to disgrace me.

I had wanted to bash Right's head into the wall when he, after seeing me adamant over my decision, said in anger that it was good that I had lost my story because if success had come to me, it definitely would have destroyed me much more than failure was doing. I didn't care as in a few days' time, I was going to head back to Lugaar. Once Ed was back from his shoot, I was going to bid goodbye to one and all.

Two days later, Jonathon found me completely inebriated on my bed. I opened my eyes feeling someone's presence around me and saw him with his hands over his waist. I got up asking him what he wanted.

"I went to Robert Smith's office yesterday evening. He is looking for you. You were supposed to report to him in a month."

"Are you trying to make fun of me?" I asked, irked. "You are well aware that there is no book now."

"But there's no harm in meeting him once. You should at least convey your message."

"To hell with everything."

"Buddy, you must at least go to him once. Maybe he can do something about it."

"Do what, huh? Do what? Is he a cop, or a detective, or a fairy godmother who with divine powers will grant me my wishes?" I asked theatrically.

"Being angry is not going to solve your problems."

"You better shut your mouth and walk away."

"Look, Charlie. I know you are sad and not in your senses and that's why you are misbehaving, and that is certainly why I am taking it so calmly…but for once listen to me and please go meet Robert."

"What sense does it make going to him to apologize for what could not happen?"

"Dude look, at least go once please. I beg of you."

"Leave me alone."

He tried holding back his anger, pressing his jaws. "Fine. As you wish."

He started to storm off, but I called him back.

"Can you find me a job, Jonathan?"

"At this point of time, my company is letting off employees. I don't think they will hire new ones unless the situation gets better, Charlie."

"Okay, can you let me know when there is one?"

He nodded his head, wanting to say something, but choosing not to. As soon as he started leaving the room, Right-Left and Max entered the room with large brown packets.

"We found a new food shop today and thought we'd try it out," Right said, lifting those packets, showing us the name printed on them.

"Great." Jonathan patted him on his back as they all sat around me on the bed one by one.

"So, what's up?" Max said looking at me and then at Johnny, swallowing half of the burger in his first bite.

"Can you arrange a job for Charlie?" Johnny said.

"What sort of work you are looking for?"

"Preferably a salesman," I said.

"Recession has made things worse, Charlie," he replied, finishing the burger in the second bite itself. "There isn't honestly an organization that's supporting intake for salesboys as of now."

"But if you want something else, maybe I can help you out in that case," Left said.

"Something else?" I asked.

"Like you can work as a labourer with contractors or so."

"Oh just shut up, Left," Right yelled. "I know what you are talking about. You want him to work for Amador. They will make him dangle on ropes and he will be cleaning the windows of buildings."

"I don't mind that, honestly." I said, wiping my face.

"No way, buddy," Max said. "No way are you going to do that. Just give us a little time and we shall definitely find something better for you."

"Please guys," I said, snatching a slice of pizza from Left. "I will be really grateful to you all."

"Come on, Charlie, since when have we turned into any lesser than being brothers that you have to be grateful to us?" Right said.

"It's not that, buddy. I don't feel good about myself. Maybe if I get busy with something, I will be able to forget Aster."

"Charlie, if you don't mind, can I say something?" Max said.

I nodded, though I was pretty sure I was not going to like what he had to say.

"Why don't you start writing again? It gives you endless joy, and during your writing days, you were so happy and impeccable in everything that you did."

"I am sorry but it is something that will never happen now. Never."

"Please, just once, for all of us."

I got up without replying and came out into the balcony. It was an orange sky in the north and the sun was on its way to the other world. The cackling of kids, the increasing noise in the streets echoed in the air. With tears in my eyes I looked at where Aster had hugged me for the first time. Why could everything not happen like it was supposed to be? Why could it not last forever? I loved Aster. I loved her so much. With every passing moment, I wanted to be with her more than ever, but the agony of the fact that I couldn't probably give her a better life killed me inside. I asked myself and God why I couldn't in an evening like this envelope myself in the warmth of Aster's love. Why couldn't I dream of spending my years with Aster being her perfect man and be perfectly capable of giving her all that she deserved?

That night was even more painful than the regular nights that I spent yearning for Aster. Nights when I would cry missing her, not knowing what to do and eventually sleep drenched in my tears. But that night, that night I was so badly missing her that I tried to lessen my pain by imagining putting my arms around her, crying and promising her a million times that I would not walk away again. I wished it could have been true. I wished for the door to open with Aster standing on the other side, telling me how she knew why I had done all that to her! And then I would have hugged her tight and never let her go. Never.

For a moment I decided going to Aster and apologizing, but then my courage vanished at the mere thought of looking at Aster's face and having to answer her questions. I rushed to the bathroom as I felt bile rising in my throat. Somewhere inside me, there was a portion that earnestly prayed to God for help me do something. Something to get me out of this unbearable pain I was slowly drowning into.

The next day came and it was no different. I was fighting a war with my thoughts and it wasn't until everybody had left for work that I tried one last attempt to sleep. I had managed to doze off in the early afternoon when there was a knock on the door. I went to open it and found Jonathan standing with somebody who had his back to me. It was when this person turned to face me that I realized to my horror that it was none other than Robert Smith.

"Can we come in?" Robert asked, sliding to the left of Jonathan.

"Please," I said, opening the door wide and letting them in.

"What is he doing here?" I whispered into Jonathan's ear as he passed me, but before he could reply, Robert called out to me.

"By the way I was really hurt to hear that your laptop got stolen," Robert said, seating himself on a chair.

I nodded my head.

"Jonathan told me everything about you. With that being said, can I please have a few minutes of your precious time?" he said.

I stood there, frozen, imagining what he must have heard from Jonathan. Robert pointed towards the opposite chair inviting me to sit down. I took the seat without thinking twice.

"I am technically a literary agent, but besides that I write, or I should say I used to write till a few years back. Now I am more into editing stuff and no writing. Evidently you too have stopped writing, so can we have this conversation as fellow ex-writers?"

"Maybe you want to interview me and write a tragedy to replenish you career, huh?"

"Obviously not," he said roaring with laughter. "Well, you seem to have been knocked about a lot, haven't you?"

"So sympathetic of you to say that," I said in anguish.

Jonathan, who sat beside him widened his eyes at me, trying to gesture at me to not be rude.

"Look! I liked your synopsis, kid, and those three chapters as well. You have it in you to go a long-long way."

"But for that my fate will have to shower luck on me, don't you think so?" I said trying to control my anger.

He nodded his head and remained busy staring at his feet, and when he was entertained enough, he asked, "Can you tell me why you were writing your book?"

"But you just said that Jonathan had told you everything about me."

"I won't surely mind if you repeat."

Letting out a big sigh, I said, "When you love someone, you try to offer the best to them. My book was an attempt to give Aster a better future. She came into my life at a point when it felt as if I was in middle of a storm and despite shouting for help, no one turned up. But just when the cracks began to widen in my boat and drown me in the waters, she came and held my hands to safely get me to the shore."

"Then why did you leave that hand?"

"Because that storm was taking her in too."

"You know what, Charlie, you cheated on her. She came to save you, but when she needed you, you ran away because of your fear and your insecurities."

"You are nobody to judge that," I said. "Love is about sacrifice. I sacrificed for her."

"You sacrificed nothing for her. In fact, you sacrificed her, and there is a big difference between sacrificing for love and escaping adversities."

"What?"

"The trouble is that we all argue to be a polymath about the theme of love, without knowing how vast a feeling it is. We make choices guided by our presumed and overrated understanding, forgetting what exactly the nub of human nature is."

"What are you talking about?" I was getting mad at him for prying into my personal life.

"What I mean is, two people don't fall in love to seek a comfortable life. It isn't a game of lottery where you are testing your luck. People fall in love to be earnestly guarded during the worst of times. And the most beautiful part about it is that lovers don't seek any guarantee from each other for satisfying them in bed or getting them all the luxuries which they themselves aren't capable enough to have. Love is the assurance that even if death stands in front of you, your loved one will hold you and love you until you gasp your last breath. That's how simple a thing it is."

The truth of Robert's words felt like the pelting of heavy stones.

"We all promise when we are in love that we will grab stars and the moon and present our loved ones with whatever they want, but later the warmth of love starts declining. What does this exactly mean? That we were lying to them in the first place to have an escape from our bad life or that we were intimidated by our limitations later? The sad part, however, is that they fall for us with utmost sincerity, but we…we either slap them with our reality or hurt them with our silence."

"Look, I agree with your viewpoint. But I'll have to say my case was an exception. I want Aster to have a good life which I can't give her," I said resignedly.

"Why can't you give her a good life? Maybe you don't have anything today, but your efforts will guarantee a bright tomorrow."

"Efforts? Didn't I make one?"

"That's the problem," he said, "You just made one. It only took you a few months to write a book. How many do you think would have gone in re-writing it? Tell me. You didn't look at the positive that you already had an agent representing you. You chose to see the negative part and hid behind it because you didn't want to work hard. Had your love been true for her, you wouldn't have abandoned her."

He had raised the tone of his voice dramatically. "You would have rewritten the book. You would have turned up and told me to give you more days. You gave her up because you are a selfish and a coward orphan. You simply used Aster to fill the gaps that your parents left. Nothing else."

I began to think hard. Robert's words seemed to be choking me all of a sudden

"Had she been in trouble, would you have only tried once or twice or thrice and said, look she is supposed to be dying so let her die because I tried and cannot do it more as I am sure I will fail? And then walk away leaving her to die alone? If that's the love you had for her, then you are the most pathetic creature I have ever seen in my life."

I was sitting in guilt, cursing myself for what I had done. As my friends had said, I was a victim of my own damn thoughts.

"What have I done? I am so sorry, Aster. I am so sorry," I was crying miserably over my foolishness.

"It's no use crying, kid. You ruined your life without even having an enemy. I pity your existence."

"No, Robert. I will write again. I'll write my book once again. I can't let her go."

"I don't think you will, Charlie. You are just pumped up by the heat of the moment. That's who you are."

"I don't want to give you my word because that's futile to me. But what matters to me is Aster. And now when I know I was wrong, I won't let her go. I won't."

"Are you sure about that? Is that what you are going to do?"

"I am not lying, Robert," I said.

"If that's the case, then I have got news for you. I had presented your stuff to one of the big publishing houses of our country, and he is quite interested in publishing you. Here is the printout of the email I received from them." He took the paper out of his bag and dropped it into my lap.

I looked at the page. The letter was a surety to publish my manuscript. I could not believe it. The letter read that they were looking to publish something on the same topic and were encouraging writers to scribble on it. Now since they had got hold of one, they were excited to read the complete story and take it forward.

"Take these three chapters of yours," he said, dumping the file in my lap. "Complete the book and come back. Let us see how much you love your girl."

"Do you have a spare laptop or a typewriter?" I asked.

He smiled at me, getting up and said, "Yes, and you are welcome to have either of them."

Assumptions are like potholes on the path of human endeavor. I wish I had gone to Robert in the first place. Had it been so, things would never have become so ugly. I regretted that I had not walked up to him and instead had taken a pathetic decision on my own.

After Robert had left, I immediately went looking for the diary that Aster had gifted me. It brought back the memories of love that I saw in her eyes, making me feel like an emperor and also reminding me of the indelible faith she had in my potential.

I flipped the cover and revisited the message she had written for me.

I sighed as I read the words. I was missing her like hell and at the same time, cursing myself for throwing away the best thing that had happened to me. My entire life, I kept craving for a family, but when God had given me one in the form of her, my insecurities and fears won over my love.

Why had it been so difficult for me to infer that she didn't crave for solace in luxury? She simply wanted a life with me. Had money been her priority, she would have said yes to Pebbles long ago.

I recalled what Jonathan had said to me once during our initial days of friendship, 'A girl doesn't want to be with a guy who is rich, she wants to be with a man who is perfect at heart – one who is honest, who genuinely cares for her, one who loves her wrinkled face as much as he admires her youthful smile. My girlfriend and I don't go to the best of restaurants, but we spend heavenly moments whenever we are together. A few drinks, a few laughs, and some moments of pain. That's all you need. It's the bond that matters which knits you as a single soul and if we share it, we must preserve it. If I calculate what I give her or what she gives me, it would be a transactional pursuit and that is not love by any means."

I finally understood that love by no means is a medium of entertainment, but a source of strength, power, inspiration and everything that's magical. I wish I had understood this long before, but all of us, do we really realize the value of people, of things, of love, or friends before we lose them? Probably not.

I started writing the story once again. My mind and my heart weren't together because on the one hand I was swept by this feeling of guilt and on the other, I was avid to meet Aster as soon as possible. However, it didn't take me much time to re-invent myself and get back to writing my best. Once I knew I had to get to her fast, I was doing my work at an unbelievable speed.

Time flew quickly. Twenty-seven days later, I lifted my finger high up in the air and pressed the last full stop of the story, feeling like a soldier coming out victorious from a war. The book was finally done and without causing any more delay, I rushed to Robert with the printouts of my finished manuscript.

I knocked half-opening his door.

He was occupied reading something very serious. His table was stacked with papers and books. A pencil played between his fingers as he read.

"It's me, Charlie," I said entering his office.

He took off his spectacles and asked me to take a seat as he closed his book.

"So young man, what would you like to have? A glass of wine or a chilled bottle of beer?"

"I am done with it," I said.

"Done with?"

"The story…the book, I mean."

He threw a look at the calendar hanging on the wall to his left.

"It's not even a month."

I passed the papers over to him. He wore his spectacles and ran through the pages, flipping through them at rapid speed.

"That's fucking unbelievable," he remarked. "You are a genius."

I didn't reply. "Anyhow, I'll take my leave," I said.

"Alright, but I'll pester you in a few days," Robert said while examining me from top to bottom. Perhaps he was checking whether I had lost my mind.

I nodded my head.

"I have one request to make." I hesitatingly said before leaving.

"Sure."

"I understand that publishing is a slow moving industry and it takes months to see your book in print, but can you somehow get it out at the soonest?"

He bit his lips, his glare stationed at the papers.

"I know I am asking for something big. But if it is possible, please do me this favour."

He smiled. A smile that almost meant sorry.

I got up and almost opened the door for leaving when he stopped me saying, "I was wondering if you would like to work for me?"

I was taken aback for a moment.

"What sort of work?" I mumbled.

"I need a creative writer for a magazine I am about to launch."

"Are you sure?"

"Yes. It will pay you three hundred pounds every month, and am sure about your growth as well."

"I...I have never worked for anything like this before. I wonder if I am the right man for it."

"Trust me, you are the best I can get. If you feel I am paying you less, I can consider that though."

"No, it's not about the money," I stood thinking for a while. "I don't want to bring a bad name to you. I fear if my work is shoddy, and would you know...."

He laughed.

"Your book is being represented by the best agent and published by the best publishing house and you are still nervous about writing!"

I smiled. "Even I don't understand that."

"Don't worry. We do have a team that will take care of all the mess you may create with words."

"Are you sure? I mean...umm..."

"You are taking the job. And I am not asking you, I am telling you this time. My secretary will send you a letter of intent. Go through it once. That's it."

I nodded, half-smiling.

Was I dreaming? My skills could earn me a job? It made me feel good. In fact, great! I was finally going to be a writer, almost had a decent job and now the only thing I needed was Aster's forgiveness. Life would be perfect then.

"Reaching home, I was crazily surprised when the door was opened by none other than Ed, who was back from his work. He looked thoroughly transformed. Classy clothes, a new hairstyle... and he smelled so awesome. I jumped to hug him, and it took only a fraction of a second for me to break into tears. All that had been building up inside me came out instantly.

"You are back!" I shouted in joy. "And you know what, I wrote the novel again. It's getting fucking published!" I said in his face, shouting even louder.

That evening closed with the biggest celebration. We owed a lot of our success to Max, Jonathan, Eugene and Benoit as well. They had not only let us share the flat with them, but had helped us at every juncture we needed them. We were truly lucky to have met such wonderful people in this city.

Three days later, I received a call from Robert asking me to meet him in his office. According to him, it was time to make things official. He had fixed up a meeting with the publisher's representative to sign the contract for the book. I read those terms and conditions and put my signatures across, receiving an advance cheque of two thousand pounds in return. All this had happened because of Aster. She was the one who brought me back to writing and I wanted to do something for her. As soon as I got the money, I rushed to buy a ring for her.

I walked into Aster's hospital braving everything that usually scared me. She was busy and seemed to be completely occupied with taking care of the patients. I kept looking at her for as long as it was possible. I wanted to say sorry right away. I wanted to say sorry for breaking her heart and making her feel so alone. I wanted to promise her that I will love her more than anything else in the world and be by her side till the end of time.

But I walked away. I walked away not wanting to bother her at that moment. I would return shortly. It was just a matter of a few more days. I was going to come back.

The guys tried to explain that I was being a fool waiting for the right moment to talk to Aster, but what they didn't know was that I wasn't necessarily looking for the right moment, but the courage to walk up to her.

What could I have possibly said to her? That I had the final epiphany and I was back for her so let's pretend that I never broke her heart or was cruel to her and go back to being normal again? There was also the fact that Aster was a gem and any guy would be lucky to have her in their life. While I lagged behind searching for confidence, there was a possibility that somebody else would have entered her life. So I was back at the hospital the next day to talk to her.

I saw Aster coming out of a room. At a snail's pace, I started to walk up to her, but just before I could reach her, I saw a tall guy approaching her. I froze all of a sudden, not knowing why.

The guy seemed to be completely charmed by Aster and I noticed how he found reasons to touch her and Aster too seemed to be very comfortable in his company. I didn't know whether I should be angry at the guy or myself or be sad at the prospect of losing her again.

Unable to take it anymore, I walked out of the hospital before Aster could see me in such a pathetic state. I was about to hire a cab back home when my newly-bought phone rang.

"Hey Charlie! It's Robert. There is a little problem that has cropped up. Can you please hurry up to the office?"

"What's the problem?" I asked in shock.

"Please reach soon.," he said. "I'll let you know."

When I reached office, Robert was already there, waiting for me. He asked me to follow him while walking away with long strides. I had to practically run to keep up with him.

"Robert, what's going on?" I asked.

He didn't reply and kept walking faster.

"Robert, what's going on, damn it. Tell me."

He still didn't reply.

Chasing him, I entered a room that was pitch black and I couldn't see anything anymore. I hated what was happening and it was pissing me off.

"What the hell is going on?" I was about to break into tears.

The lights turned on. I looked around. All my friends were standing, clapping and hooting for me and a big poster of my book was being displayed in full length on the screen. Robert grabbed copies of my book and handed me one. I stood frozen.

He shook me, pulling me out of my reverie and I glanced at the copy of my work that Robert had just placed in my hand. I was holding the gist of my entire life in them. All my agony, desperation and fatigue seemed to melt as my work sat right in my hands. It was unbelievable.

The cover page was so lovely. It depicted a girl sitting in dark with her face hidden, and below, my name was printed – CHARLIE.

I flipped its pages and the smell of the book to me was like a child's first breath. It wasn't still sinking in.

"We have scheduled to release it three days from now."

"Why have you done so much for me, Robert?" I asked in astonishment.

"I see so much of me in you."

"But what makes you think that we are the same?"

"You didn't read my novel ever. Did you?"

"No."

"Yeah, it was such a disaster. But read it. You will find the answer," he said with a grim expression. "Plus, I was only able to sell a few copies, so if you buy it, I'll sell one more."

"I am not buying one," I said. "You are gifting it to me."

"So I lost a potential customer, huh?"

"I thought we were friends."

"By saying that, you just ruined your chances of being adopted by me."

And both of us laughed, looking at each other.

"Alright, foster dad," I said hugging him, controlling my tears.

So it was final. My novel was going to be released after seventy-two hours. The media was contacted and all the local newspapers were supposed to be covering the news of its release. I wanted to run to Aster. I needed to show the book to her and fix everything and moreover, it was her who was going to release it. Even if she had moved on in her life, I wanted Aster to be right by my side when the book released. I owed it to her. It was she who had pushed me. It was she who had ignited that fire in me. I didn't care about what I had seen at the hospital, or what the past had inflicted. All I wanted was for Aster to release my book. I was even ready to beg if I had to.

I ran to the hospital as fast as I could.

I wasn't able to find Aster anywhere in the hospital so I stopped one of the staff passing by and asked. "Sir, can you please tell me where I could meet Miss Aster Rembert?"

"You are referring to the medical student?"

"Yes."

"She has gone to attend a medical camp in Lugaar."

"And when is she supposed to be back?"

"I don't exactly know," he answered. "But they will take a month or so, I guess."

"Are you sure about it, and when did she leave?"

"I am sorry, sir. I don't have that much of information."

"Fuck!"

"What?"

"Nothing."

I immediately called Ed and told him that I was leaving for Lugaar, and would positively return before the ceremony. He offered to accompany me, but I refused saying that it's just a matter of two days. Moreover Robert would definitely need someone to make all the arrangements, so it was better if he stayed back and helped him.

The line at the ticket window was exhausting. The train for Lugaar was supposed to arrive in the next twenty minutes, and it was the last one for the day. I felt miserable standing there. "Why do I encounter obstacles in my path all the time?" I wondered for a moment.

I was still behind thirty to forty people in the queue when the last train for Lugaar entered the station. I had had enough of standing in the queue and finally decided to board the train without a ticket, no matter what the consequence would be.

I got into an almost empty compartment and occupied the first empty seat I could find. The train slowly moved out of the station and picked up speed on its way to my destination. Barricades, trees, farms flashed past me taking me back to the memories when Ed and I had come to Etiole in a train like this. Back then, had somebody predicted this day for me, I would have laughed it off and called them lunatics. But how unpredictable life really is! Good times were going to be a matter of a few more hours now, I knew.

The night was growing older, but there was no sleep in my eyes. The lights inside the boggy had been switched off and I could hear the sound of so many people snoring and farting at the same time. It seemed like people were taking serious undue advantage of the darkness.

I laughed pressing my novel under my arms and lifted my knees on the seat as the temperature kept dropping. The steady rolling current of air swayed my body and I was shivering in the cold. Physically, I was in distress, but mentally, I was happy. Very happy.

I stepped down at almost every station where the train stopped, anxiously waiting for the whistle to be blown and signal to turn green. Most passengers waiting for their trains on the platforms were sleeping or ready to doze off.

The sun started coming up but Lugaar was still twelve hours away, and to make it worse, the train had started to stop every few minutes for no apparent reason. I wondered why, after going through all that I had to, God was still adamant on testing me.

"Okay God," I said in my mind trying to strike a deal with God. "Do as much as you want to do it, but please, when Aster and I are together, just be good to us, forever, and I promise that we will thank you each day for the rest of our lives."

Exactly at 8:00 a.m., the train stopped at the railway station of Lugaar after a delay of almost eleven-and-a-half hours. It was a bright sunny day with the sun beginning to spread its heat. The fragrance of snacks, the voices of the newspaper boys and water boys welcomed me home. I saw that the ticket window was empty, so I bought two tickets back to Etiole for that evening for me and Aster.

It was a bit of a struggle, but eventually I had managed to get all the information regarding Aster and her group in Lugaar. I headed to the hotel where the entire batch was staying. And on the way was the bakery where I had worked for seven years of my life. He (the bakery owner) was sitting outside his shop, twirling his moustaches, enjoying the sunshine with a newspaper in his hand.

"The Mou-Man seems to have got no older, huh?" I said as I neared him.

"My boy!" he smirked and stood up opening his arms to welcome me.

"It's been so long," I said clinging to him in pure affection.

"I cannot tell you how great it is to see you," he said. "Where is Ed, my notorious delivery man?"

"He did not come this time, Tommy. But will surely meet you soon."

"What's that book in your hand?"

"It's my book."

"Of course it's yours, but I meant what is it about?"

"No, I mean I have written this book. I authored it."

"Are you trying to fool me or what?"

"See the name on it, Tommy," I said, handing him the book.

He was evidently shocked, but at the same time he was extremely joyous.

"Jesus Christ! You have pulled off something incredible," he said, repeatedly flipping through the book.

"Tommy, I was wondering if you would like to come along with me for the launch of this book."

"It isn't in the market yet?"

"No Tommy, we are launching it day after tomorrow."

"I wish you all luck in the world, my son."

'So you aren't coming along?'

"It's impossible for me to leave the bakery," he said. "Especially when I don't have good boys like you anymore."

"Okay Tommy, I'll take a leave now, but I'll come back again."

"Don't forget to bring Ed along."

"Certainly not." I said, taking my leave with a goodbye hug.

I reached the only good hotel Lugaar had and asked the girl at reception about Aster's room number, and requested her to let me have a word with her. It took a bit of pleading and begging, but she eventually dialed the number to Aster's room. There wasn't any response.

"Sir, I am sorry but Miss Rambert isn't picking up the phone."

"In that case, you may tell me her room number. I can go and check. She is my fiancé," I said.

"That's…"

"Charlie?"

I turned around. It was Isabella.

"Oh! Hi Isabella. How are you?"

"Perfect. I am quite stunned to see you here."

"Yeah! It's quite sudden, I suppose," I said. "I hope the honeymoon went off well?"

She smiled from the side of her mouth, as if it offended her.

"I apologize," I said wondering whether I had offended her in any way. "Maybe that was too personal."

"No. Don't... don't apologize. The fact is we are divorced."

"What?"

"Yeah. It happened within twenty days."

"I am so sorry to hear about it."

"It's okay. Forget it."

"But yours was such an extraordinary wedding," I said. "All I could think of was you and William being happy forever, cherishing the memories of your wedding day, having a wonderful family life…"

"When a girl makes the mistake of being with a hypocrite, this is what it leads to."

"He cheated on you?"

"He had many affairs. Anyway, let's not talk much about it. What about you? What are you doing here?"

"Where is Aster? I came here for her. She isn't picking the phone?"

"She left early in the morning with the professor to ensure all the arrangements were in place. We have a camp for the underprivileged near Queen Hill today."

"Oh!! Okay. Do you…do you think she'll forgive me?"

"Forgive you? Forgive you for what?"

"The way I treated her," I stopped for a second. "Didn't she tell you anything about what happened after your wedding that day?"

"No! She only said you were writing a book and would be back in a month or two."

"Sorry?"

"Yeah! Like you were facing this writer's block and needed some time alone to get back to your form."

"She said that to you?"

"Word to word."

"Oh my God!" I went down on my knees with my hands covering my face, regretting that she had not even blamed me for what I had done to her and that she believed that I would be back because she knew I loved her.

"Is everything alright?" Isabella asked, keeping a hand on my shoulder.

"Not as of now, but I am soon going to make it perfect," I said looking into her eyes. "And thanks Isabella. I need to go now, I'll meet you later." I got up.

And as I turned to move out, I heard the ear splitting sound of guns being fired.

"Terrorist attack?" I thought in my head, my heartbeats getting frightfully fast.

The sound then suddenly grew into an explosion, breaking the window panes of the hotel. A piece hit Isabella under the ear. Dreadful panic ensued. I checked on her as she immediately broke down. There were echoes of clamoring and babbling. Another big noise of a blast followed. I ran to the door to check and I could see a large group of people in black clothes with faces covered, firing down blindly and throwing bombs in every direction.

They began to run abruptly to their right, but firing still.

"They are heading to the Queen Hill." I realized. Plus, it was the ideal place to do the maximum damage.

"Holy Shit! Aster is there."

I ran out fast and jumped over that lengthy ramp, surviving a collision with a car that was coming towards the entrance of the hotel at a very high speed. I regained my balance, without entertaining the cries of Isabella asking me to stop.

The sound of the bullets did not halt. Not for a fraction of a second. Every noise was like a signal of someone's death. People were losing their lives. Their cries had instilled fear everywhere and for everyone around.

"This can't happen, this can't happen," I constantly murmured as I ran through the valley towards Queen Hill. Evil images came before my eyes and I couldn't stop my tears from falling. I prayed to God that there was no need to give Aster to me, but just save her and let her live, let her smile and let her grow old peacefully.

Meanwhile, the sound of blasts and guns kept compounding. Apprehensions began to batter my mind.

Eagles flew over my head in the direction I was going. There were bodies of people who had been shot in my way. All of them looked so horribly repugnant. They were either shot in the head or in the face. Some had bullet wounds on their chests, stomachs, knees and legs. It was pure chaos. A deplorable image slipped inside my brain where I was shouting after locating Aster among all the dead people.

I shouted my nerves out, *"It will not happen. No!"*

And then a bullet came flying from above the mountain, hitting me in the shoulder and making me fall down on the ground. My book fell right next to me and the two tickets to Etiole inside them slipped out. I looked above and it was a man firing wildly in my direction. A rain of bullets came sucking the life out of me and I felt the world turning into a pit of black and drowning me in it.

Time and terror have one thing in common; when they aim for you, they are strictly merciless. And both had hit me together.

I had always heard that life flashes by when you die, but for me, the only one thing that flashed before my eyes was Aster. Fate had always toyed with me and I was never its favourite child. Else I wouldn't have died miles away from my girl. The car that I had avoided getting hit by was bringing Aster back to the hotel and though she never saw me in the midst of all the confusion and chaos, it was Isabella who told her that I had come to see her, and she instantly knew that I had come back for her.

But along with that, she also realized one more thing. That I just might run very-very far from her. And how could she let me do that! She stood almost dead listening to Isabella, but immediately turned and ran for me, breaking through all of security, military or whatever that had come. She did not care for anyone who shouted or tried to stop her. Because she was in pain, but her love was far deeper.

Falling again and again, getting up each time still and yelling my name trying to stop me, she found me on the ground with blood all over. She screamed, falling on her knees near my body recognizing me and having no courage to turn my face towards her. She was shivering in complete disbelief, crawling away, biting herself and sobbing harder.

I had never ever wished for anything as badly as for a tiny little breath so that I could say sorry to Aster. I never wished to leave this world with the regret that I was the one who broke Aster, in spite of knowing everything that she had been through in life. I wanted to scream and yell. If I could hold Aster and tell her that I came back for her, came back in a hope of having a family together and that for me there was nobody else but her and it would remain so forever. But nothing could help me now, for time and fate had yet again tricked me by snatching away the one thing I had wanted so badly in my life.

When I was alive I had made her cry, and now after dying, I was offering her nothing but agony and memories drenched in pain and tears.

Aster saw my book lying to her left somewhere, and noticing my name printed on its cover, she opened it quickly. She saw her name there on the first page. It read:

Dear Aster,

Thank you for teaching me that anybody can steal my work, but nobody can ever rob the feelings with which I write them. I promise you a million times that I will never discontinue writing. Because of the words you said, the time we spent, the love we had, the pain we shared, I have been able to pull off this dream of writing a book.

I love you from the core of my heart, Aster. You are the reason I am. You are behind everything good that has happened to me: this book, this moment and the life to come. I can survive being a captive in a dungeon but I cannot live without you. You complement me. You complete me. You are my drug. You are my angel.

I love you.

Always yours,

Charlie

She sobbed harder reading it and her cries echoed in the hills louder that the sounds of bullets. She jumped on me, hugging me and crying for me to come back, but I was long gone. Perhaps her cries were too much for the gods to handle, as a rain of bullets was showered upon Aster, and she died too.

♦

Edwin rushed to Lugaar as soon as he came to know about our deaths. He took my head in his lap and sat stiff, declining to believe that I had died. How could he have believed it when every smile we carried and every tear we cried had been shared by us right from the day when we were little kids? He could not accept that the boy who used to tell him each and every single detail of his life had left this world without caring to inform him. We had seen every dream together, painted every single fantasy with our arms across each other's shoulders. And now, all that he was left with were the memories of those days when we used to laugh at each other's idiosyncrasies.

I wished that I could lock him in my arms and say that I'd meet him soon and to take care of himself.

"You made me an orphan once again. Why did you do that, brother, why?" Ed cried, performing my last rites along with all my friends.

For many days that followed, he refused to eat, drink, sleep and do anything except sit in a dark room and cry. And on many nights he would go and sit under the bridge where we once slept, recalling the moment when we promised we'd live together in that apartment.

He refused to appear for the promotions of his first movie, saying that since the one who wanted to see him doing it was no more, he wouldn't do any of it. He found life difficult and it took him almost a year to come to terms with destiny.

After five years, *The Crumbled Gender* was acclaimed as an international bestseller. It became the fastest selling book in two countries.

That same year, this novel was adapted into a movie and coincidentally, I was honored with the best story writer for it. My share of profit from book sales and rights were used by Ed to set up an NGO that worked against molestation of children and women and also set up a forum for budding writers. He took care of my purpose as he kept me alive in his heart.

Every night I came along with Aster, swirling in the endless sky to say hello to our friends: Max, Jonathan, Eugene, Benoit, Claire, Ed and the cute little baby in his arms – Charlie Perrod.

An orphan who came all alone in this world had left, making the most beautiful bond of friendship.

How lucky I was!

Eleven Years Later

"The winner, ladies and gentlemen..." The lady says as she has finally decides to reveal the best actor of the year.

"...the man of the moment...is...*Edwin Perrod!*"

The stadium fills with echoes of joy and hooting. Every single person gets up on their feet to applaud for my friend. But he has covered his face with his hands and is inconsolable. Claire too has tears in her eyes but she is trying to calm Ed. She is telling him that he needs to get up and walk to the podium. He nods his head, wiping his face and hugs her tight before he begins to walk to collect his award.

I too am clapping for him just like all other friends of his: Jonathan, Max and our very own Right-Left. Ed collects his memento and has the microphone in his hand to thank the world.

He takes a deep breath and looks up at the sky. I don't think he'll be able to speak. He is crying like a kid and so am I. But he gathers himself gracefully, takes a deep breath again and says, "Like every artist who grows up to live this moment, I too grew up with a dream to lift this in my hand. But this isn't exactly how it was supposed to be…because the one who would have been happier than me, torn my ear drums shouting in joy that 'I told you, I fucking told you that you will be living this moment' isn't alive today. However, I am sure that in some form or the other, he is here, smiling at me, clapping for me and telling me to not miss him. But man, I want to see you too. Be with you one more time and relive my childhood in that dark orphanage where we found life in each other. Trust me, those were much better days than where I stand today. You know, every moment you spend with the people you love is more precious than the desires you wish could ever come true. I love you Charlie – my brother, and I miss you every single moment I breathe. If possible, please come back. I find life meaningless without you. I miss you…I miss you…."

With tears in my eyes, I turn back and walk wondering if there would come another day when I would run to my friend and hug him like I used to, and would there be another birth when both of us would meet again?

Recommended Reading

You Are The Best Wife

Ajay Pandey

This is a true story of two people with contradictory ideologies who fall in love. This is a story of the author after his beloved wife left him halfway through their journey. This heart-warming tale of a boy and a girl who never gave up on their love in face of adversities, ends on a bittersweet and poignant note as Ajay comes to terms with the biggest lesson life has to offer.

An engineer by degree, Ajay works in the IT field and loves to read and trek. He has immortalized his life story through this book.

ISBN: 978-9382665540; Price: 175/-; Pages: 248; Binding: Paperback.

I Still Think About You

Arpit Vageria

For Aamir, little Dhruv is the best gift life has given him. More than just brothers, they are the beginning and end of their family. After years, struggles and pain are slowly fading away in the face of happier times when suddenly everything is thrown into darkness and pain.

This is a story of love, brotherhood, passion, dedication, pain, and the depths to which a heart can go to win back lost love

Arpit writes scripts and more for the Indian television industry, and enjoys road trips, singing, and adventure sports.

ISBN: 978-9382665700; Price: 195/-; Pages: 185; Binding: Paperback.

It Doesn't Hurt to be Nice

Amisha Sethi

Kiara is a dynamic, thirty-something girl who has reached great heights professionally, and is the apple of the eye for almost everyone who knows her. But she never took any short cuts.

More than Kiara's story and the wisdom she achieves through the various dramatic and hilarious experiences of her life, this book is a motion picture with you in the lead role, perhaps a 2.0 version of you.

Along with holding top notch positions in leading companies in the past thirteen years, Amisha has also done extensive research in ancient scriptures.

ISBN: 978-9382665489; Price: 175/-; Pages: 144; Binding: Paperback.

A Broken Man

Akash Verma

Krishna is a Dalit boy from Bihar who falls in love with Chhavi, a high caste Brahman girl propagating equality in a politically charged Lucknow University campus. Their love is ruthlessly crushed by a society that thrives on divisions of caste and religion.

This book is the quest of a deprived Krishna to redeem hope from despair, love from separation and success out of repeated failures.

Akash Verma is an entrepreneur and has published two bestsellers till now. He is fascinated by cinema, literature, history and travel.

ISBN: 978-9382665694; Price: 195/-; Pages: 240; Binding: Paperback.

The Pleasure is all Mine

Shanaya Taneja

Trisha wants to be rich and famous, ready to open her arms to people like Sanjay, who have trophy wives to show, and dirty secrets to hide. Bharti feels Sanjay's love has vanished with time, and finds herself unable to resist Ankit's lovable charm.

A story of love, lust, deception, dark and dangerous pleasures, and betrayal, this is an irresistibly sensual page-turner that explores having it all, and the consequences of wanting more.

Shanaya is an advertising professional who loves to read romances. Her observation of people reflects how the cost of love is the highest of all.

ISBN: 978-9382665724; Price: 175/-; Pages: 176; Binding: Paperback

---

Stupid Cupid

Ankit Sonthalia

Unlike various students who have their dreams sorted out, Suhaan likes to "go with the flow". It's only when he starts playing cricket for the college team that he realizes his passion. But then, cupid strikes. He is reveling in love and dreams of a happy life when he is asked to choose one – passion for cricket or love for Namrata.

Will Suhaan make the right choice or will life once again call the shots for him? *Stupid Cupid* is a tug of war between dreams and love.

Ankit Sonthalia runs a construction business and is married to his childhood love interest Ankita. He is fond of travelling and exploring new places and does it often.

ISBN: 978-9382665717; Price: 195/-; Pages: 144; Binding: Paperback